One Day *Life* Will Change

a story of love and inspiration to win
life when it hits you hard . . .

Saranya Umakanthan

PASSION

Reprint 2022

FiNGERPRINT! **PASS!ON**

An imprint of Prakash Books India Pvt. Ltd.

113/A, Darya Ganj, New Delhi-110 002,
Tel: (011) 2324 7062 – 65, Fax: (011) 2324 6975
Email: info@prakashbooks.com/sales@prakashbooks.com

facebook www.facebook.com/fingerprintpublishing
twitter www.twitter.com/FingerprintP
www.fingerprintpublishing.com

ISBN: 978 93 8971 784 6

Processed & printed in India

To Lord Shiva -

The powerhouse of energy,

The symbol of permanency,

The lightness and the darkness,

The divine love,

The world, The Universe,

The one who has shown me that

miracles are indeed possible;

The one who'll stay with me forever and beyond;

I owe everything I hold precious to you;

And that includes my writing;

I love you Shiva. Om Namah Shivayah! Har Har Mahadev!

CHAPTER ONE

THE END

‿

When life tosses lemons at you, squeeze them!
God is fed up of hearing your whiny "Why me?"

Samaira observed the flame flickering in the corner of the house. The cluttered two-bedroom apartment in Chennai never felt like "home." The pale-yellow light from the *diya*[1] did its final dance and waned off, highlighting the finality of her situation. Her fingers trembled as she signed the papers. They say that life begins at twenty-five, but for her, it was the end. The deed was done. She packed her suitcases and took only the bare necessities that were hers. Uncertainties loomed ahead, threatening to push her into darkness. Unconsciously, she tucked her hair behind her

---

1   A small cup-shaped oil lamp made of baked clay.

ears. Wearing a simple cotton *salwar*[2] suit, she had no idea how innocent she looked. Without thinking, she had chosen a black dress that day. Except for the small gold hoops on her ears and a wristwatch, she had left all her jewellery behind, as they were not hers. Beads of sweat dotted her forehead. She had to face it; there was no other way. She never wanted to see him again for as long as she lived. Walking out with an air of finality, she took a local bus to her mom's place. The bus was empty.

Like my heart and life . . . her mind taunted her.

"Damn," she cursed herself. Her self-esteem was at an all-time low; Ashish had made sure of that. The pathetic part was that she was aware of it and yet, had allowed it to happen. Taking a seat next to the window, she closed her eyes. Her cheeks were wet. Tears still clung to her eyelashes. She had tried her best to make this relationship work but it had been a lonely and uphill task—with no help from the other side. Theirs was a typical arranged marriage based on a perfect horoscope match. Ashish's mother had looked for a fair and slim bride, and she had fit the requirements to perfection. Her glossy hair and sharp nose enhanced her beauty. The dimples in her cheeks charmed everyone. Little had she known that her angelic looks had lured her into the trap. After their engagement, they had chatted and dated. It was the sweetest period of her life, and she had fondly imagined Ashish as the prince of her dreams. She

---

2   A pair of light, loose, pleated trousers, usually tapering to a tight fit around the ankles, worn by women from South Asia typically paired with a top called the *kameez* to make a *salwar kameez* suit.

remembered the times when she had slept with the mobile phone sandwiched between her ear and the pillow. And she had cherished the heart-shaped pillow he had gifted her. Her treasure box was filled with his gifts . . . teddy bears, mugs, and dried roses. She had cherished those little treasures like crazy. Their marriage ceremony was a grand success. Surrounded by uncles and aunts, the occasion was filled with fun, frolic, and lots of food. Of course, her dad had footed the bill for it all.

But barely a week after the wedding, everything had changed. The honeymoon was over. She saw the other side of him. He had forced her to quit her career as an IT professional on the first day of their marriage and made sure that she was confined to the kitchen. Frustrated, she found her only relief in singing. She had loved rhythm and sound even when she was a kid. Her excitement and joy towards her passion were brutally killed by him. He had scraped out her feelings and mocked her talent. His words had hurt her so much that she had given up singing. Her heart lingered on that painful day, reminiscing.

It was dinner time, and her forehead was beaded with sweat.

If the *rotis*[3] turned out rough or were not served hot, Ashish would throw his plate at her. His mother would then make a big scene acting as if he had not eaten for years. Samaira wanted to throw the plate back at him, but her innate politeness stopped her. She would never sink that

---

3   Indian flat round bread cooked on a griddle.

low. However, she made sure that her *rotis* came out soft and served them hot. Engrossed in her task, she hummed a melody; she was not aware of it until the voices from the dining table reached her.

"Thinks she is the top singer," mocked Ashish.

"Ha-ha, more of a bathroom singer," her mother-in-law remarked.

Ashish smirked. "Good-for-nothing."

"Her tone is raw, and her rhythm is completely out of place. Had my music teacher heard her singing, she would have slapped her," his mother said, revealing her singing expertise. She cleverly hid the fact that her teacher had chucked her out of the class after the first week.

"Ask her to stop singing . . . or I will puke," he ridiculed.

"I will end up with indigestion," she added.

Samaira stopped in her tracks. She rushed out of the kitchen and ran into the bathroom. These horrible people should never see her tears.

"See what you have done," his mother wailed.

"What?" Ashish demanded.

"Who will make our *rotis* now?" she grumbled.

Furious, Ashish banged on the bathroom door.

"Where is our dinner? If you don't come out now, your divorce papers will be waiting for you," he yelled.

Samaira came out quietly. Her face was blank. She had wiped her tears. She served the steaming *rotis* to the selfish people who manipulated her.

For the sake of her parents, society, and the institution of marriage, she had put up with almost everything for the past two years, tagging it under the label of "adjustment."

Nevertheless, things never changed; to be precise, her husband . . . now ex-husband . . . had never changed.

She had thought that having a baby would change him, but that did not happen. Samaira was blamed for that. "Barren land" was the nickname given by her mother-in-law, and she had stopped criticising when Samaira fortuitously discovered Ashish's reports, which told her otherwise. Though it shocked her, she tried her best to stand beside him. She cared more about his health, but Ashish did not see it that way. His psychosis grew, and life became intolerable. He stayed out and did not come home most days. Finally, when he brought his girlfriend home, completely drunk, Samaira decided that she had had enough and could not take this anymore.

"I want a divorce."

Samaira's voice shivered as she made the demand the next morning. Ashish and his mother stared at her.

"Is this how an Indian girl would talk to her husband?" his mother shrieked.

"Is this how an Indian son would behave after his marriage?" she shot back, pointing to the girl who slept peacefully on his bed.

"He is a *man*," justified his mother.

"Is he?" Samaira scoffed.

A dig at his manhood, Ashish raised his hand to strike her.

She caught it, saying, "Enough, Ashish! Hit me and I will drag you to the police station for domestic violence."

Her sharp voice made him take a step back. She turned to his mother. "All I want is a divorce and nothing else. Don't force me to do things that I don't want to do."

Having never seen that avatar of Samaira, her mother-in-law agreed to a mutual divorce, knowing that her son was in the wrong. She wanted to hush it up so that Samaira did not drag things out in public.

Her parents were blissfully unaware of her sorrows and Samaira had made sure that it stayed that way. With the divorce papers in her hands, all she wanted to do was bury her face in her mother's lap and howl like a child. The bus stopped at Anna Nagar.

The moment she reached her house, Samaira realised that something was not quite right. Her uncle Ram and aunt Pariti stood at the door. Ram was her father's younger brother. Though they had talked occasionally with her over the phone, she had not seen them after her wedding. Garlands of roses adorned the entrance. Her neighbours hovered outside.

"Samaira, where did you go?" Her uncle rushed to meet her.

"Uncle . . ." she fumbled and was lost for words.

"We have been trying to reach you for more than two hours, but your mobile was switched off."

"Is something wrong, Uncle?" Samaira demanded. A cold and weird feeling took hold of her. Her intuition warned that something was desperately wrong.

"Err . . ." her uncle stammered, raising her anxiety.

Pariti ran to her and cried, "We have lost your parents and your brother, Samaira. They met with a car accident."

She stood shocked. Seconds ticked by. There was no response from her.

"Samaira." Pariti shook her shoulders.

Not my parents . . . not my brother . . . there must have been a mistake . . . her heart argued.

"No, dear," Pariti stressed.

Waves of sorrow hit her. "Oh my God!" Samaira staggered, unable to digest the fact.

Are these people playing a prank on me? She did not want to believe it. No . . . no, this was not happening to her. It could not be, but everything around her was real, though it appeared surreal.

"How could God snatch them away? They had many years left with them," her aunt continued miserably, and her wail tugged at Samaira's senses.

Her family had left her in darkness. No Mamma . . . no Pappa . . . and her strong brother who had appeared invincible was no more. The truth hit her hard.

The plug to her consciousness was pulled and just like that, Samaira fainted.

"Bring her some water," her uncle screamed.

"Relax, Samaira; you have to stay strong. There are certain things that are beyond our control," her uncle's voice brought her back to reality after a couple of hours. She felt completely drained and just nodded. The house was jam-packed with her relatives, and she wanted to shoo them away, but she did nothing and felt nothing. Nothing seemed tangible and she felt frozen inside. The last rites and formalities were done. Sitting in the corner of the house, she did not shed a single tear.

She imagined that once everyone left, her Mamma and Pappa would walk in as usual. Her Mamma would make her favourite coffee and her Pappa would take her for a drive in his car to the beach. She would fight with her brother for the front seat. They would have fun together, and she would build a sandcastle for them. They would all be a happy family just as they used to be.

"What are you going to do?" her uncle's voice broke her reverie.

Samaira observed him blankly.

"Come on, Ram, tell her!" Pariti pushed her husband.

"Tell me what?" Samaira queried softly. She had received the worst blow of all, and nothing could hurt her anymore.

"Your mother and father left you debts," her uncle informed her with pity.

"Which they borrowed for your wedding and your brother is no more," reminded her aunt.

"You are responsible for their debts. I got a call from the bank. You owe them Rs.30 lakhs," Ram told her.

"You have an option, Samaira." Pariti's words were firm, compelling her to accept the reality. Samaira strained to grasp her aunt's words.

"Sell the house to us; we will clear the debt and deal with the bank; won't we do this for our sweetheart, Ram?" she tugged at her husband's shirt.

Uncle Ram looked embarrassed. There was guilt written all over his face.

Samaira remembered her dad's words that their apartment was worth at least Rs.60 lakhs. But that did not matter now. Monetary benefits meant nothing to her. She nodded in acceptance.

"Okay, then . . . we will get the papers ready." Pariti pulled her husband onto his feet. She wanted to wind up this deal before someone else could sweet-talk Samaira out of it.

"Let us leave the girl in peace. She can clear the rest of the stuff. Take your time, darling. You can move out after you sign the papers," Pariti said, sounding magnanimous.

"Take care, Samaira." Her uncle gently squeezed her hands, reluctant to leave her alone.

"I will," she confirmed.

"Did you hear that? I know that Samaira is a strong girl. Come on, let us go." Her aunt patted her shoulder.

It was over. Why had no one inquired about Ashish? Her mind was baffled as she stared into the empty space around her.

Did it mean that everyone knew about her divorce? She pushed that thought aside. She did not care. The house was bare and eerily silent. Reality slowly sank into her. She was alone now. No family. No parents. No money and not even a home. She was virtually penniless, and vultures surrounded her.

She would have to talk with her mother . . . tell her that she had no one . . . and that her aunt was cheating them on their house. She laughed at the irony of it and lost her composure completely.

"Oh God, where has my life gone? Where is my Pappa?"

"Mom, where are you?" She broke down and flopped down on the floor, thumping her fists on the ground. Her cries echoed around the empty house. She sobbed miserably. Her tears drenched the floor. Hours passed. God had not only snatched her parents away but had also taken her younger brother with Him.

"How dare He!" She punched the floor with her hands again. Bouts of hysteria attacked her. Her heart bled as she reminisced over the moments with her brother.

"You went back on your words, bro. You told me that you would get me a new dress with your first month's salary, but you left me before you even got it!" her voice broke with a loud cry. She screamed.

"Why is life so unfair to me?"

"And why only me?"

Had God counted the number of times humans had asked him this question, it would have effortlessly surpassed the biggest number on Earth—googolplex!

CHAPTER TWO

STUMPED AGAIN

Difficulties are for betterment. They stump, twirl, batter,
and knock us down, but they also polish us, and we begin
to sparkle like gems at the end of the course.

Samaira stepped into the marriage hall. It was her
cousin Sharmi's wedding. She was not in the mood
to join the occasion, but Sharmi had begged her
to come. A month had passed after her parents'
tragic death. Nothing seemed permanent. She
had to hand over the property documents to
Uncle Ram. They went ahead with the wedding
despite her parents' death. She did not mind that,
but her heart ached as she remembered how her
dad had been waiting to see Sharmi all dressed
up as a bride. A wave of loneliness enveloped her
as she walked in. Her relatives acknowledged her
reluctantly with a half-smile as she strode past
them. But their hushed voices the moment her

back was turned caught her attention. She was standing beside a pillar with the papers in her hand, deliberating whether to call her aunt, who was busy attending to the guests.

"It was not an accident," Pooja's voice stopped her. She was their neighbour.

"Not an accident?"

The response was from an unfamiliar voice. Samaira assumed that she must be one of her distant relatives. She recalled seeing her with her mother a year ago.

"Yes, that is what they say."

"Who are 'they'?"

The same question hovered on the tip of Samaira's tongue.

Pooja ignored the inquiry. "That is not important. What matters is, Samaira's parents committed suicide." Her voice sounded malicious.

Samaira was stunned.

"How do you say that?" the other woman inquired out of curiosity.

"Samaira is divorced. Ashish did not attend the death formalities."

"What does her divorce have to do with their death?"

"Her parents were worried thinking of their daughter's life, and her father's concentration was never on the road while taking that turn. As a result, they went under the truck and her brother paid with his life for her sins."

Samaira felt suffocated as if a ball was stuck in her throat.

Was it true? she wondered. She had kept her divorce a

secret. They would not have known about it. The rational part of her brain protested to her heart.

"She ditched her husband and killed her parents," Pooja declared mercilessly.

"Oh my God!" Samaira cried.

They turned around as they heard her whimper. The other woman had the grace to blush, but Pooja said, scornfully, "What is there to cry about? It is the truth after all."

With those words, she moved away to share her gossip with her other friends.

Had her dad found out about her secret? If so, what they said was true. She had killed her parents . . . and inadvertently her brother too.

How could you? she asked herself. Filled with self-loathing, she walked into the restroom. The mirrors mocked her.

"She killed her parents . . ." the words taunted her. Is that what the world believed about her? If her parents had lost their concentration because of her, she would never forgive herself. She shook her head in anguish. Her head pounded; holding the iron bar close to the washbasin, she attempted to steady herself. Her knees were wobbly. She had to leave the place.

The papers from her bag fell as she turned away from the mirror. She had almost forgotten the reason for her visit—to give her uncle the property documents. As she came out of the restroom, her uncle saw her.

Acknowledging her, he moved closer and held her hands. "Are you okay, Samaira? Your eyes are red."

He looked at her sympathetically.

"No, I am okay. The property documents."

"Hold on; why the hurry?"

Just then, the bride waved to her from the *mandap*[4].

"Hah, Sharmi wants to meet you. You go to the stage. Say hello to your friend. Apply some *haldi*[5] and come back," he teased her.

"Are you sure, Uncle?" confirmed Samaira.

"Don't you want to do it?" he demanded. Her lips curved upward. Sharmi's infectious smile caught up with her.

"May that smile always stay on your lips," her uncle blessed her and patted her shoulders. She went to the other corner of the *mandap* and took some *haldi*. When the crowd gave way, she moved near Sharmi and stood opposite her. She did not notice Sharmi's mother-in-law on the other side, with the gossip-loving Pooja. When she was about to apply *haldi* on the bride's cheeks, she was stopped.

"How dare she?" Sharmi's mother-in-law-to-be screamed.

Aunt Pariti rushed to the *mandap*. Things were getting beyond her control. This marriage must happen at any cost. Her daughter's future was at stake and this was a wealthy alliance too good to miss.

"Yes, she is right. How could you?" She turned to Samaira with her hands on her hips looking angry.

Holding Samaira's hand, Pariti crushed her fingers, forcing her to drop the *haldi*. Samaira's fingers trembled in pain.

---

4   A temple porch (in southern India).
5   Turmeric.

"Auntie, I don't get it," her voice quivered as she looked at Pariti's angry face.

"You are a divorcee," she condemned.

"At least *you* have some sense," the mother-in-law applauded.

"Do you want Sharmi to inherit all your bad luck?" Pariti said, fire blazing in her eyes. Samaira looked around with embarrassment. Everyone's attention was on her. Uncle Ram came to her rescue.

"Pariti, it was me; I told her to—"

"You stop your nonsense!" she burst out. Samaira's heart wept silently.

"Don't you want Sharmi to be happy?" She grilled Samaira again.

"I want her to be happy."

"Should she end up as a divorcee like you?"

Pariti's stern voice tore her heart in two.

"Sorry, Auntie." Samaira tried to cover her monumental mistake.

Pariti lost her temper. "Cut out the apologies. Just leave the stage, Samaira. What you have done is more than enough to wreck this show."

Mortified and trying to control her tears, Samaira ran from the stage. The emotional drama kept the crowd entertained, and they observed her with interest.

Uncle Ram caught her at the entrance.

"I am sorry," he said.

Samaira dumped the papers in his hands. Her lips trembled. "I came to give you this, Uncle. I will leave."

Handing over the papers, she left, dejected.

Standing near his broken car on the left pavement, Vivian silently cursed.

"How long is this going to take?" he asked his driver.

"Fifteen minutes, sir."

"Damn . . . I am going to be late," he swore.

At twenty-eight, he had made it to the top in his career. Punctuality was his norm. As the boss of Creative Tanks, he had to be on time for the meeting with the managing director of *Awzome* clothing store. He was based at the Bangalore corporate office and had come to Chennai to finalise the deal and sign the one-year marketing contract for the huge multiple-store outlet. He had started the company from scratch, and there was no way he was going to allow it to dwindle away because of a flat tyre. His trip could not end in vain. His frustration did not affect his classic good looks. He was dressed formally in a blue three-piece suit and polished leather shoes. At twenty-eight years, over six feet tall with broad shoulders, he always stood out in a crowd. His olive-tinted skin and toned muscles were a testament to his regular workouts. His broad face and sharp jawline gave him the perfect look of a Greek God but with straight black hair.

Shaking his head, he was about to hail an auto when his black eyes clashed with dewy brown eyes, glittering with a shade of honey. That was the moment Vivian saw her for the first time. She walked on the pavement, towards him. His hand stopped in mid-air. But her eyes looked beyond him. She had not noticed him at all. Hypnotised, he stared at her and his brain rang warning bells to his heart.

His *own* angel! Vivian frowned.

Now from where did that thought come? He had no time for women. They were a distraction. But his heart resolutely refused to obey.

Samaira did not know where she was going. Her knees ached from tiredness, yet she kept walking. The dizziness pushed her off the footpath. Her mind, heart, and body ached. Her soul felt as though it was ripped from within her. She wanted to pour out all the pent-up tears of a lifetime, as she crossed the road. She swayed, and her legs faltered.

She paused, holding the lamppost for support. Steadying herself, she continued her aimless journey.

Is she okay? Vivian speculated, staring at her.

She walked past him. His eyes took in her graceful movements. He breathed in her feminine, floral perfume.

Plop! Something fell on his right hand, and he raised it to examine it.

Droplets of tears!

Why the hell was she crying?

Vivian was annoyed. He hated losers. But hatred was not what he felt right now. It was something else, and he did not want to put a name to that emotion, which took root powerfully in his mind. He wanted to hold her, cuddle her, kiss her, and tell her that everything was going to be alright soon.

What is wrong with me?

His self-condemnation did not stop his pulsating heart. She was merely a stranger. And he would probably never set eyes on her ever again. That thought brought out his sourness. Irritated, he turned to the other side. He had an urgent business meeting to go to, and he must *not* entertain distractions. That was just what she was. A beautiful distraction.

"Sir, the car is ready," his driver called out to him.

"Good," he acknowledged and opened the door. It was time for him to leave. His head turned of its own accord, to get a glimpse of her for the last time. She was walking towards the right lane. He had the impression that she had no destination in mind. Though she was physically present, Vivian was sure that her attention was elsewhere.

Samaira paused for a second. Her right ankle hurt. She bent down to examine it. A tiny pebble was stuck in her slipper. A wry smile hovered on her lips despite her tears. Balancing herself, she strained to get rid of the stone with her left hand. She was oblivious to the fact that she was in the middle of the road.

She had no idea of the monster of a yellow lorry cruising towards her, well above the permitted speed limit. As she was on the other end of the road, she would not be visible to the driver. Vivian's mind alerted him of the impending danger.

"*Arre* . . . lorry," he warned her in a gruff tone. Though she was close enough, she did not hear him. Shaking his head, he ran towards her. There wasn't much time and his only thought was of her safety. It was a narrow road, and within a matter of seconds, Vivian covered the distance between them. His heart was in his mouth. As he grabbed her and pulled her to the other side, they fell together, with her toppling over him.

"Do you have a death wish?" he demanded.

Breathless, Samaira did not reply. She could not comprehend what had happened. The road was deserted, except for two people who were in deep conversation in the other corner.

"Are you okay?"

She raised her head and gazed at him but did not reply.

Vivian lost his flow of words and was arrested by her hypnotic eyes. The chocolate in them drew him towards her. She seemed weightless. Her velvety softness felt like a feather against his hard chest. Her brows were perfectly arched, and her mouth was full like Cupid's bow. She lifted her hand and brushed off a lock of hair from his forehead.

What is she doing? His breathing became erratic and he found it difficult to control his desire. Her fair face was flushed and partly wet.

He believed that she was attracted to him as well. This was the wild moment he had waited for in his life. And that beautiful moment was going to be with this girl. Irrationally, he felt somehow connected with her. Her magnetic gaze untied the cords in his heart. Her lips trembled, and his heart pounded like a drum. He was oblivious to where he was and raised his face towards her. His lips longed to meet hers.

"Bro," she said, and that wild moment crashed around him. It was as if someone had poured a bucket of ice-cold water on his heated body, and the splash of reality hit him.

"You came back." She gently traced her fingers along his cheeks. "Please don't ever leave me again, bro. Bring Mamma and Pappa with you. I need them. I beg you. I swear that I will never fight with you."

Vivian was moved. It seemed like she was in the midst of an awful tragedy in her life. But this should stop. Then she bent down and gathered him close.

He gasped. He realised that the girl assumed him to be her brother. Grabbing her by her shoulders, he shook her hard to bring her back to her senses.

But his efforts were futile. Her wounded eyes revealed her affection for the brother she had lost.

There was only one option left to bring her back to the living. He did not think of the repercussions of his action. He pulled her close and held her cheeks. Tilting her face, he kissed her hard on her lips. His body shuddered at the electrifying heat that coursed through his body.

Samaira came back to her senses with a jolt of shock. She looked at Vivian.

"Oh my God!" she cried. "What are you doing?" Then she looked at her state and stammered, "What was I doing?"

Realising she was partly lying on him, she pushed him away. Guilt rocked her, and her face became red with embarrassment.

"I am not your bro, and never will be," Vivian said, wryly.

Noting her surroundings, she stood up quickly. She had to leave now. She could not stay here a second longer. But his intensely spoken words broke her.

"Who asked you to be?" she retorted and walked past him.

Vivian sighed in frustration.

CHAPTER THREE

THE TURNING POINT

Life can either be a misery or a miracle.
It is up to us to appreciate the enchantment in our
lives or hide behind the curtain of gloom.

The desire to survive waned. Completely fed up with her life, Samaira cursed the person who saved her. He should have left her to die. How did her muddled-up brain imagine him as her brother even for a moment? She should have known that her brother would never come back . . . just like her parents. But they were at least together. If not for that man, she would have joined them. Her anger doubled. She hit her forehead in despair. Not content with taking everything from her, God would not even let her die quietly.

How pathetic could it get? Self-pity coursed through her, and she shivered hysterically. She had kept walking, and the office-going crowd now dominated the road. She checked the time. It was almost 9.30 a.m. She had woken up at 4.00 a.m., considering the early *mahurat*[6] of her cousin's wedding. Traffic was at its peak. The red signal halted the vehicles from the other end for more than a few minutes.

"What happened?"

No one knew.

"*Ma*[7], I am going to be late for school," a little girl complained, seated behind her mother on their bike.

"Don't worry, darling. I think everyone will be late. Ms Sadana is visiting Chennai today."

That explained the rush on the road. Sadana was an influential politician from Karnataka. Samaira caught the woman's eye and nodded in understanding. The woman responded with a smile. As she walked along the pavement, the traffic was the least of Samaira's worries. She had other things on her mind. A sharp cry halted her. It was the pathetic moan of a woman. Samaira looked at the crowd, wondering what the commotion was all about. A man stepped out of an auto, visibly sweating. His taut muscles revealed the tension within him.

"How long are we going to stand here?" he demanded the auto driver.

"Sir, I think it will take some time. Ms Sadana is crossing this way," the driver answered helplessly.

"Damn her," he cursed. It might take aeons just to get

---

6   An auspicious time for an enterprise to begin or for a ceremony to take place.

7   Mother.

out of the traffic. Bending back into the auto, he reassured his wife, "Don't worry, darling; we will reach the hospital soon."

The pregnant wife sobbed, which pierced the hearts of all the onlookers. The auto driver shook his head. It was beyond his control. They were stuck in traffic. Her innate thoughtfulness led Samaira to help the woman. Two more women joined her.

"*Anna*[8], don't worry. The traffic will clear soon. I will go and check with the police over there," Samaira calmed the husband who looked helpless and frustrated.

Holding her nine-month tummy, the woman screamed in pain. The baby was due any moment now.

"Please do something," she begged her husband. In response, he kicked the road, showing his resentment of the situation. The woman Samaira had seen earlier joined them.

"Sona, you wait for me." She instructed her daughter to wait for her on the pavement.

"Stay calm. I am a gynaecologist. I can help," she assured the couple.

"Will you assist me?" She turned to Samaira, who stood next to them. Understanding the urgency, Samaira readily agreed. They carried the woman a little farther away on the pavement, where the crowd was minimal. Samaira lent her shawl, and the other women around them followed suit. Together, they hastily made a makeshift room, shielding the pregnant woman and the doctor, giving them privacy. The

---

8   An elder brother (often used as a respectful title or form of address).

doctor brought a medical kit from under the seat of her two-wheeler.

"Is she all right?" the husband asked coarsely with concern.

"Yes, as healthy as any of these women." The doctor winked. Samaira noticed that the wink did wonders to pacify the raging husband.

"But please calm down and stay here. I don't want a crowd inside," she instructed, expecting to be obeyed without rebuttal.

"I will help you," volunteered Samaira.

The doctor took her inside the enclosed space that they had created for the labour. Though Samaira's knowledge did not extend to medicine or treatment, there was a rapport between her and the doctor. Her temporary job was to follow the doctor's instructions to the dot.

"She needs help right now," the doctor told her.

The expectant mother rolled in blinding pain. "Hold still," the doctor told her.

"What is your name?" Samaira asked the woman.

"Radha," the woman mumbled.

"Relax, Radha, we are here to help you," Samaira reassured the woman, who was in no mood to listen. She was in agonising pain. She squeezed Samaira's hands as she experienced her next contraction.

"We do not have much time. Her uterus is dilated. The position is perfect. The baby might be out any moment now," the doctor told Samaira after a quick examination.

She observed the mom-to-be, who had calmed down for a moment after the last contraction. Radha sweated profusely and was as pale as a sheet. Samaira mouthed reassuring words to her, holding her hands. The doctor did her job with equipment that Samaira could not even name. To top it all, she had a flask of hot water as if she was equipped for an emergency birth.

"Don't look at me like that. That was for my daughter. I did not plan this," she smiled, as she took some water out of it.

Thank goodness! She is in safe hands, thought Samaira, admiring the way the doctor took over this emergency and her memories transported her to her pregnant mother. She had been five then.

She could still recall the sound from the adjoining room at home. Samaira had waited with her father outside. The screams had scared her as a kid. She was frightened that something had happened to her mom. Her grandmother and doctor were with her mother. The little yell from her brother had put an end to her mother's cries. She had delivered the baby even before they had time to take her to the hospital. It had been an emergency birth. There were multiple complications after that, which they had not shared with her as she was too young to understand.

Radha's moan broke her reverie.

"The next contraction is coming. Be prepared," the doctor warned.

"Forewarned is forearmed."

"Make sure she does not flip over in pain," she instructed Samaira.

"Now push," she said, turning to Radha.

She panted and wriggled to push, without any success.

"Come on, you can do better than that," urged the doctor.

Samaira whispered in Radha's ears, "You can."

"Think of your baby . . . your beautiful bundle of joy. Don't you want to see it soon? Its tiny fingers and toes . . . push harder," the doctor encouraged her. At her next contraction, Radha shoved the baby with all her might, and they all heard the much-awaited tiny cry.

"Bravo!" the doctor applauded. She cut the cord.

"Look at your angel," she prompted Radha, who was drained completely. With tears in her eyes, the mother saw her daughter in wonder.

"Naughty girl . . . couldn't you wait until Ms Sadana passed this road?" she chided in mock anger. Samaira laughed. The traffic started moving again. She cleaned the baby and passed it to the anxious father waiting outside. The crowd cheered and whistled.

"My clinic is close by. You can take them there. I will join you quickly," the doctor informed the husband. He rushed to his wife's side, holding their precious baby. Her worries forgotten for the moment, Samaira congratulated the doctor for handling the situation efficiently.

"It was my pleasure to bring a life into this beautiful world, and it is my job," the doctor brushed off the compliment modestly.

Radha's husband called out to Samaira.

"My wife wants to speak with you," he informed her and turned to the doctor to express his gratitude. Acknowledging the doctor, Samaira went inside.

"Thanks . . . what is your name?" Radha's voice wobbled.

"Samaira."

"I am indebted to you, Samaira. You were a pillar of strength throughout. Without you and the doctor, I would never have seen my little girl. Look, how beautiful she is . . . her eyes . . . her hair."

Samaira smiled at the pride in her voice.

"Hmm, you are going to be a doctor in another twenty-five years and help women like me, got it?" she ordered the little one.

The baby whimpered. "Look, Samaira, she says okay," the mother said.

***

Samaira ordered coffee at the café in the corner. Her thoughts went back to the baby girl and the mother's struggle to bring her into this world. She could still hear and feel her cries. Despite all her troubles, Radha wanted her baby girl to be a doctor in the future. Birth was truly a miracle. That thought broke Samaira. She wiped her tears. She decided she was not going to cry anymore as she realised how stupid she had been.

"Even my mother faced this crucifying pain to bring me into this world. She would have envisaged a future for me . . . just like that mother . . . and all the mothers in the world," whispered Samaira to the empty space around her.

She would not want to see me dead . . . wherever she is.

Her thoughts guided her in the right direction.

Whatever happens, I will not destroy her dreams, and I am not going to throw away my life; it is a gift from my mother.

Samaira's heart reiterated these words as thoughts of suicide flew out of her mind. She acknowledged the waiter, who placed the cappuccino in front of her. Life was waiting for her.

***

It was almost a week after his Chennai visit. Vivian was back in Bangalore with the signed deal. He led a disciplined life and had enjoyed success throughout. Though the initial phase of his growth was tough, he had learned from every obstacle and situation. He should have been elated with this deal, but he felt strangely deflated. The mesmerising brown eyes of the girl haunted him as soon as he closed his eyes. The worst part of it was that he did not even know her name.

The chilly December weather had prompted him to dress warmer than usual. The grey blazer he wore with his white shirt matched his pants. His secretary walked into his cabin.

"What is up, Raghu?"

"Vivian," Raghu stammered. The company encouraged employees to call each other by their first names and followed an open-door policy. Right now, Raghu was not comfortable in sharing the news with his boss, because he could predict his reaction to it.

"The general manager, marketing . . . he is in hospital," Raghu informed Vivian.

"How serious?"

The look on Raghu's face revealed all.

"Oh God! Make sure that the company bears all the medical expenses, and forward three months' salary advance to his family," Vivian instructed his secretary.

Frowning, he asked, "He looked okay to me . . . how old is he? Thirty-two? Thirty-three? What happened to him?"

Raghu dreaded that question.

"Attempted suicide."

"*What?*" Vivian rose from his chair.

"Vivian, he had issues with his wife ever since their baby was born. I believe that family pressure and depression made him—"

Vivian signalled to Raghu to stop. He did not want to listen to the sob stories of losers. To him, whatever the problem was, suicide could never be a solution.

"Give him three months' pay. But I don't want him in my company anymore," he commanded, brooking no objection.

"But, Vivian—" Raghu began to protest.

"Creative Tanks is not a place for losers; this is the place for fighters—either we swim or sink!" blasted Vivian.

Knowing that Vivian's decision was made, Raghu did not press further. He knew that it would be like banging his head against a stone wall.

"Anything else?" asked Vivian, raising his eyebrows.

"Yes, we have a candidate waiting to be interviewed for the IT Specialist position in our marketing department, but we just fired our manager, right? What do we do?" Raghu replied sarcasm tinging his voice.

One could never change Raghu. Vivian almost smiled.

"When is my next meeting?"

"In half an hour."

"Hmm, so it is not a big deal; send her in. I will interview her," Vivian informed him.

Giving his boss an appreciative glance, Raghu nodded. He would do anything from A to Z for CT. Work was Vivian's girlfriend. That thought drew a teasing smile on his lips.

"What is so funny?" demanded Vivian.

"Nothing . . . I will send her in," he replied dutifully.

"What is her name?"

"Samaira."

***

There was a knock on his door. Vivian shut his laptop after verifying the signed deal of his contract with *Awzome*.

"Come in," he invited. He had forgotten about the interview.

Raghu ushered Samaira in and Vivian was dumbstruck for a moment. It was the same girl he had kissed and declared that he would never be her brother! The moment she stepped in Vivian knew that fate was playing a different game with them.

"Samaira, you are lucky to be interviewed by the boss himself. Meet Mr Vivian Andhera. Vivian, this is Samaira Ranjan," Raghu made the introductions.

Their eyes clashed. Samaira jerked with a flicker of recognition.

"We have met," Vivian revealed.

Samaira willed him not to reveal the whole story. This

was her first interview, and she needed to get this job. Raghu's eyebrows lifted with interest.

"We met on the road, Raghu. We did not have time to introduce ourselves. Am I right, Mr Andhera?"

She fielded that one brilliantly.

"Yes, Raghu, that's true. We were busy with other things," dragged Vivian on a playful note. Samaira could not meet his eyes. The secretary watched them with curiosity.

"Anyway, let us begin the interview, Miss Ranjan. Please be seated," Vivian concluded his conversation with Raghu.

***

Samaira dutifully passed on her résumé to Vivian. She had applied for the post of IT Specialist. Except for good marks in academics, her résumé did not have much in terms of professional experience.

"So, Samaira, you are a computer science engineer with a year of industry experience, and that was two years back. Are you not working now?"

She drew in her breath. She knew she could not evade the question—any interviewer would have asked the same.

"Yes, I was working until I got married." She paused.

Is she married? Vivian felt as if he was punched right in his stomach. But she was not wearing a *mangalsutra*[9]- on that day or today.

"Then I was not allowed to work."

---

9   A necklace worn by a Hindu woman to signify that she is married.

Even to her, the excuse sounded feeble.

"By whom?"

"My hus . . . ex-husband," Samaira said reluctantly.

"Oh." There were a thousand questions Vivian wanted to ask her, but professionalism stopped him.

"And you let him dictate to you?"

"Not anymore . . . I am free," came back Samaira.

"Good. We don't want submissive people here. We want people to speak up even if their superior is wrong," Vivian told her, matter-of-factly.

"I will, sir," declared Samaira.

He liked her determination. They were interrupted by a knock.

"Sorry to bother you, Vivian, but we have to send the new tag line to the *Awzome* marketing team today. Our team has finalised one, and they wanted your confirmation. They had sent you an e-mail, but you probably did not see it, what with the interview."

"Hah, yes, Raghu. Give me a moment, Samaira," he said.

Samaira liked his courtesy. She observed him surreptitiously. His glossy jet-black hair was well-groomed. His attractive eyes complemented his physical fitness. There was not an ounce of extra fat on his body. He exuded strength. He caught her looking at him.

Samaira bent down quickly averting her gaze.

What am I doing? she chided herself.

For God's sake, pull yourself together, Samaira . . . isn't one bad experience more than enough to haunt you for the rest of your life? she told herself.

But the only thing she could not understand was, how did she even mistake Vivian for her brother? She must have been too groggy. But not groggy enough, because her heart still remembered their stolen kiss. A wave of heat snaked through her body. Though she had boxed it into a one-off incident, reminiscing about that moment made her blush.

Vivian lifted his eyebrows inquiringly. Samaira shook her head in confusion. He quickly went through his e-mail and read the tag line aloud.

"*Awzome Clothing—the Beauty and the Best.*" Vivian frowned.

"That sounds bad," opined Samaira.

Raghu gasped.

Vivian turned to her. "Is that so?"

"Yes."

"Justify, Samaira."

Not sure whether she was doing the right thing, Samaira said, "Sir, *Awzome* clothing store is about men's clothing. They have not yet ventured into women's clothing. So, this tag may not attract men, I believe."

"Hmm, what do you suggest then?" Vivian did not take his eyes off Samaira.

"I can tell you that what you have chosen is not going to work. Given time, I think I can come up with something else. In this case, the tag line should be more oriented to comfort rather than beauty."

Raghu stood speechless. This girl had put down the entire team with her argument. He was fascinated to see how Vivian would react to this.

What she said made sense to Vivian. He turned to

Raghu wordlessly. Raghu got the message, nodded, and left, closing the door after himself. The tag line was condemned.

She waited for the verdict with bated breath.

"But, Samaira, for an IT specialist, we need someone with at least three years in the industry," informed Vivian out of the blue.

Hah, that is it! My interview has gone for a toss . . . he is trying to sugar-coat his words to send me away. Her thoughts went volatile.

With anger exploding within her, she got up from her chair and said, "I understand your decision, sir . . . I will leave."

Frustration welled up in her. She began to walk away when her right leg collided with the left leg of the revolving chair, and she fell. Vivian rushed to her; she lay on her back.

"Come on, Samaira, falling down seems to be a habit with you." He laughed.

Not in the mood to take a joke, she said, "It is not. You pushed me the last time."

"Yes . . . true. If I hadn't, you would not be here now," he mused as he pulled her up, holding her hands.

Dejection enveloped Samaira.

"Yes, I would have died. I would have thrown away my mother's gift, my life, because I did not care . . . I didn't want to. I am doomed to fail in everything I do, just like this interview. I am failure personified, and no one wants to be with me—not my ex-husband, not my parents."

Vivian did not expect that angry outburst. She appeared calm and composed on the surface. How did he not realise that underneath that quiet exterior, a volcano waited to erupt?

Samaira gasped as she covered her mouth. What had happened to her? Getting rejected in the interview was one thing but thrashing the interviewer and pouring out her sob story was unprofessional. The reality sank in, and she rushed out with a cry.

Vivian did not like losers, but Samaira was different.

How different he did not know, but she was his girl. His mind kept repeating that to his pathetic heart. The feeling of being connected terrified him, but he would never let her go. He never wanted to see her tears again. So, he promised, *I will never let you cry again, Samaira. Life is for living, and I will show you how. I swear.*

CHAPTER FOUR

THE SECOND INNINGS

A candle never fears being lit, nor does it say no to relighting. A beginning is always a new beginning even if it is the second or the third or the fourth.

Vivian gave her exactly one day to cool off. It was time to bring her back. Why he was doing this he had no idea. Normally, his patience did not stretch to grooming losers. But Samaira did not seem like one. When Raghu had asked for the status of her interview, he had not elaborated.

"Let me have her résumé, Raghu. I will call her."

Her temporary residence told him that she stayed at a working women's hostel nearby. Her mobile number was on her résumé, and he called her. She answered on the third ring.

"Hello, Samaira, this is Vivian from Creative Tanks."

"Hello, Viv . . . sir." Her voice was down as she heard his name.

Was it guilt? he wondered.

"Good morning. Call me Vivian . . . Creative Tanks encourages all its employees to address one another using their first names."

Why did that matter to her?

"Yes, Samaira, I called you to inform you that you are selected."

"But yesterday you mentioned that you need someone with more experience," she argued.

Had Vivian volunteered the job out of pity, she would have shoved it back in his face.

"Yes, for an IT specialist, but we want to hire you for our Ideas team; you will be managing the content for our marketing campaign. You should have waited before jumping to conclusions and storming out, Samaira."

"I apologise for losing my cool, sir; it was not intentional," she blabbered.

"Oh . . . meanwhile, we will also brush up your IT skills to get you back into your area of expertise," he added.

It sounded too good to be true. "Is this for real?" she asked.

"Walk to the office, Samaira. Sign the appointment letter and start work today."

The line went dead. She stared at her mobile phone as if it had grown horns.

***

And Samaira did just that. It was more than a month now since she had joined CT. As promised, except for the IT training for two hours, she worked for the Ideas department. Creativity was the key element there. She was mapped to generate marketing ideas for *Awzome*, and it was one of the biggest projects that the company had bagged in recent times. As the company's CEO, Vivian had taken a special interest in the success of the project because he believed that it would lure bigger brands to come to CT for marketing. Her thoughts lingered on her boss.

She met Vivian daily. Since the department manager had been chucked out, Vivian was temporarily managing that role until the replacement came in. He was a dynamo. His ideas, suggestions, and instructions were spot on. His organisation had several branches, and she worked at the corporate office in Bangalore. Samaira was lucky to have him as his mentor, and she had learned a lot from him in the short month she had been there.

Her heart fluttered with his thoughts. He made her overlook all her life-threatening woes. The work was demanding and interesting. Gradually, he was putting pieces of Samaira back together, for which she was grateful. *Was it just gratitude?* The thought crept out of nowhere.

Obviously, her brain confirmed to her heart.

"What happened, Samaira? Stuck with ideas?" Vivian asked her as he crossed by her desk.

She smiled. "Good morning, boss," she wished him.

She had come in early today. They were scheduled to visit one of *Awzome's* outlets. She had to collect inputs on the look and feel of the store and the quality of the apparel and identify their best attributes to include in their campaign.

"All ready?" inquired Vivian.

"Yeah, all geared up," she announced.

"That is my girl."

Samaira got those "feel good" vibes from him. With Vivian's compliments and appreciation, her previous failures did not loom large in front of her.

"Please wait for me in the basement," he told her.

His feelings for Samaira tied him in knots, and he was not sure where all this was taking him. But as his recruit, she was top-notch and one of the excellent resources at CT. Sometimes he even forgot that she was not from a marketing background. Her creativity was outstanding. Her fresh mind became a mandatory requirement for their latest campaign.

Vivian strode towards his car. His sleek BMW had a golden tint, which gleamed under the sun. But there was no sign of Samaira. Where did she go? He glanced around him. She was waiting for him next to the company-cab division. He sighed. She never crossed the official border.

"Samaira," Vivian called out. As he saw her coming towards him, he got into his car.

"Are we going in your car?" she asked anxiously.

"Is there a problem?" Vivian lifted his eyebrows.

"No . . . none," she stammered.

"Good! Come, let us go," he invited her in.

She was about to occupy the back seat as if the very air he breathed was about to contaminate her when Vivian lost his patience and hissed, "I am not your driver, Samaira."

Her face turned red. "No, boss, I thought Raghu will join you in the front."

"Do you see him anywhere?"

She shook her head. "But that was the plan, right?"

"Yes, that was the plan, but Raghu called this morning. His wife is sick, and I gave him the day off to take care of her. Anything else?"

How would I know that? fumed Samaira. Vivian was the dominant type. She sat beside him without a word and closed the door with a bang.

"Poor door," commented Vivian wryly.

As she turned to Vivian to make a cutting retort, he put a finger on her lips. With a gasp, she swallowed her words.

"It was a joke, Samaira. Just relax. We have a big task ahead," said Vivian.

She nodded. This was her job and she must not mess it up.

"Put on the seat belt," he instructed.

Seeing her pathetic struggle, he bent towards her to help. Their eyes clashed. Their faces were so near that Samaira could feel his breath on her cheeks. His attractive gaze drew her, and she moved towards him involuntarily. His look did not waver and kept her captive. Vivian gently pushed the tendrils of her hair beside her ear.

She did not stop him. "Samaira." His voice was husky.

The call brought her back to her senses with a jerk. Noting her withdrawal, Vivian clipped her seat belt silently. He ignored the incident and started his car.

Samaira cursed herself for behaving like a love-sick idiot. She knew the repercussions of love and did not want to fall into the same trap again. To her, love was a snare that would never let her lead a life on her own terms. Two years with Ashish had taught her the harsh realities of love and marriage.

She worried about the awkward moment that had happened a few minutes ago. Vivian's attention was on the road. Maybe she had blown the incident out of proportion.

The car stopped at the *Awzome* outlet.

"Look for inspiration," he told her.

Samaira nodded. If Vivian could act as if nothing had happened, so could she.

They moved towards the entrance, and the sensors opened the glass door. Cool, floral-scented air greeted them. Her shawl fluttered and shielded her face partly. Her vision was blocked. She struggled to remove the offending cloth and did not see the step on the way. She tripped.

Laughing, Vivian caught her from behind. She fell back on his shoulders, and he had a firm hand on her hips. "I told you, this has become a habit for both of us!"

"Don't you dare laugh at me, Vivian! I mean, boss," she fumbled as his first name rolled off her tongue.

Noting her slip, he questioned, "Are you daring the boss?"

"Yes." She did not back down.

"So, what is the plan? Throw me out of the job?"

That brought her back to reality. What was she doing? Her job meant everything to her. Why was she playing with fire, then?

Vivian understood that her mind's wheels had started to spin out nonsense and it would be tough for him to release her from the invisible cord with which she strangled herself.

"Samaira." Vivian's voice brought her back. She realised that he was waiting for an answer.

"Me . . . throwing you out of your job? Come on, sir, be realistic." She drew the official line between them firmly.

"Come in, Vivian," the store manager's voice interrupted their conversation. Vivian's eyes promised that he would deal with her later.

The outlet had been informed earlier about their visit, but Vivian had insisted that there should not be any preferential treatment. He had let them know that his goal was to get the "feel" of what a normal customer would get when shopping in their clothing store.

"How may I help you? What are you looking for?" An employee rushed to attend to them. Since it was a weekday, it was not crowded.

"I don't have anything specific in mind." Vivian's face was blank.

"Are you interested in our ethnic collection or office wear?"

"Office wear sounds good."

They were escorted to the section for office wear. The huge section had blazers, formal suits, shirts, and ties. What attracted Vivian was an area marked "For your special Fridays", which had casual wear for office. There were plenty of collared T-shirts stacked but no round-necked ones, as many offices didn't permit their employees to wear those.

Samaira observed that and commented, "Good move."

Vivian was impressed. The person who accompanied them gave them space to look at the clothes, while standing by to help them, just in case. Vivian chose a bunch of clothes and went to the trial room to try them on.

Samaira waited outside. Vivian's selection was fast, but to Samaira it felt like he was taking a long time. She glanced at her wristwatch with a sigh. Unconsciously, she began to hum a song.

Every night in my dreams . . . I see you . . . I feel you . . .

About to try on a cream-colored blazer, Vivian stopped in his tracks. Was she playing that song on her mobile phone? It did not appear so, as there was no background score. There was a pause as she coughed and then continued. She had such a beautiful voice, and there was soul in her music. He was awestruck and stood enthralled until she finished.

Vivian emerged, wearing the blazer. That was the one he liked best out of the whole lot.

Samaira turned. She could not take her eyes off him. The blazer sat on him like a second skin, and it was a perfect fit, accentuating his more-than-six-feet-tall body. Unable to read her eyes, Vivian lifted his eyebrows.

"Do I pass?"

"You are . . . I mean, this looks good on you," stuttered Samaira.

"Does that mean I did not look good before, but this blazer makes me look better now?"

"I did not say that," she protested. He looked at her intently.

"You know you are handsome."

"Do I?" he sighed. Vivian cursed silently for being obvious. When had he ever needed a girl to compliment his looks? And he knew that he was fishing for one from her lips.

"But you forgot this." She pointed to the front button of the blazer. Leaning a little, she attempted to button him up. It came naturally to her.

A man of around fifty, who stepped out of the next trial room, gave them an odd look.

"Come on, mate, don't let your wife work for you even when you are taking her out shopping. Men these days don't even know how to button their blazer . . . very bad, young man. Pity you, woman," he retorted.

Samaira blushed crimson. The onlooker had misconstrued her action. Waiting for Vivian to clear their relationship status, she was stunned when Vivian simply agreed.

"Yeah, sorry, mate . . . I swear this is the last time," he told him. The other man strode away proudly as if he had done his part to save womankind.

"Hope this is not the last time," he murmured in her ears.

The fresh fragrance of her shampoo tantalised him. Reaching out, Vivian enfolded her in his arms.

"Oh, God!"

That proximity confirmed to him that she was his woman. His wife-to-be . . . always and forever. She was created for him. With that alluring thought, he cupped her cheeks and brushed his lips across her forehead. *He sealed her fate.*

"Vivian," Samira murmured helplessly. What had happened was beyond their control. Both wondered if they had lost their senses. Before Samaira could protest, a salesgirl's voice interrupted them.

Vivian dropped his hold on her as if she were a bar of hot iron.

"Hey, Mr Handsome," the salesgirl murmured and sauntered leisurely towards him. She wore a one-piece knee-length outfit. But Samaira was quick to pick the flaw. It had an indecent neckline, and she stood barely an inch away from Vivian. She wanted to drag her face out of his view and punch her in the face.

Vivian laughed in response. "Hello there, Miss Charming," he mimicked her voice. The girl went away with a salute.

"Miss Charming? I thought you had better taste than that. By the way, I hope you understand it was a marketing gimmick," remarked Samaira, completely forgetting her earlier romance.

"I have never seen you bitchy," came back Vivian.

"Bitchy?" she admonished.

"Yeah . . . or are you jealous?"

She shuddered as she heard the word "jealous." Vivian was right. What was happening to her? Did she forget her status? She was the little orphan trying to make the best of her pathetic life. She had to be cautious. "Love" was an overrated word, and she was not even going to spell it anytime in the future.

"Jealous . . . come on, boss, you think too much of yourself," she put him down gently.

"A moment back . . . when I almost kissed you . . . it was Vivian," he pressed.

"A mistake on my part."

"You are not a child to make a blunder like that . . . you knew what you were doing, Samaira. Think about it," suggested Vivian.

He called the salesperson and requested her to pack his clothes. Paying for his purchase, they left the place in stony silence.

CHAPTER FIVE

ARGUMENT ON LOVE

Love is seeing the dreams of your partner through your
eyes and holding hands tightly on the journey
towards those dreams.

It was Saturday. Samaira rang Vivian. To her
surprise, it was her own voice as the caller tune,
the song she had hummed in the shop yesterday.

Every night in my dreams . . .

Her voice echoed in her ears and multiplied
her doubts. She had to warn him off, having made
"that" decision after a sleepless night.

Vivian frowned, sweating from his morning
workout. Why was Samaira calling him? She
never did that unless there was a pressing official
matter. And never ever on weekends.

He spoke out loud to the empty air, "As if
you don't want her to." His mind kept speculating
on the reasons before he picked up his mobile

phone. Did she feel what he had felt yesterday? Did she share his feelings and want to talk about them? The thought made him warm and happy.

"Hello, Samaira, what a surprise!" he said, taking the call. It was 7.00 a.m.

"Hello, bo . . . Vivian!" There was a momentary silence.

Vivian waited for her to continue. He knew how tough it must have been for her to break out of her shell and call him.

"If you don't have any urgent business today, can we meet, Vivian?"

"Where?"

"The Cafe Day at Whitefield road. I mean the one adjacent to my hostel; I will ping you the address."

"No need. I know the place. Catch you at nine, Samaira."

The line went dead. She smiled wryly. This was Vivian's speciality. He talked to the point—no more, no less and it made him a shrewd and successful businessman. He was a perfect example of the type of man she liked—tall, tanned, and handsome. His sharp sculpted features and his aura of mysteriousness attracted her.

But her thoughts plummeted. Images of Vivian shattered, and her memories took her back to Ashish, who had murdered her soul with his cruel games and taunts. She breathed heavily. She would never allow anyone to do the same damage again.

Her heart told her that Vivian was not Ashish, yet she could never risk love again. She was not the carefree Samaira she used to be, and she would never forget what life had taught her. She had to nip everything in the bud or both would end up getting hurt. She did not want that to happen, and she did not want to lose him as her friend.

He was the best thing that had happened to her in a long time. A romantic entanglement would spoil everything. She had to make him realise that he was her best friend . . . nothing more. But Vivian had never spoken about love. Was her mind exaggerating what had happened between them yesterday? Was she overthinking it, making a story out of a non-existent relationship? Her brain clouded with jumbled feelings.

"It is always better to clear things in the open instead of repenting later," she convinced herself and got ready for her café visit.

**

Samaira was five minutes early and chose a table in a secluded corner. Their conversation needed to be private. Vivian arrived, dressed casually in a yellow T-shirt and blue jeans. His presence dominated the room as he entered and caught the attention of everyone. He was a head-turner.

She looked gorgeous in a multi-coloured floral-patterned kurta. The gold hoops in her ears enhanced her twisted topknot. Vivian was tempted to gently push the lock of hair that fell on her forehead.

"Hello, Vivian." She waved, completely unaware of the beauty she projected.

"Samaira," he acknowledged.

"What can I get for you?" she asked him. He took the seat opposite to her.

"Chicken sandwich and a mango milkshake to begin my day."

Samaira told the waiter, who brought the cappuccino she had ordered earlier. The faint aroma of coffee taunted their space.

"I love the smell." Vivian inhaled with satisfaction.

Samaira was determined not to react to him, but his action made her smile. She tapped the table, not knowing how to begin the conversation without sounding awkward.

"So, Samaira, I never expected your call." Vivian winked.

"I have something important to discuss," she agreed.

"Hmm, I knew that. Samaira would never call me unless she's sure that the sky is going to fall," exaggerated Vivian.

Having come this far, she struggled to find the right words for what she wanted to say.

"Vivian, I must tell you I am not the one you are looking for."

"For what?"

"I am married."

"Not now," he corrected.

"And I hate love." She sighed.

"What a combination of words, Samaira . . . *hate love*." He did not even blink.

"Vivian, be serious. I am trying to tell you something."

"I am listening, go ahead."

Though Vivian tackled her with sarcasm and humour, he wondered where she was going.

"I don't believe in love," she reiterated.

"Is that your problem?"

"No, I don't want that to be a problem between us in the future."

Vivian understood. She was warning him off indirectly.

"Just answer me, Samaira. What is love?"

She laughed nervously. He did not take his eyes off her.

"Had you asked me that question three years back, I would have replied that love is the eternal bond that ties a man and a woman . . . but not now. To me, love is humbug; it means nothing . . . it pulls you down and throws you into the gutter." Her anxiety was obvious to Vivian.

"Samaira, look at me. Do you *really* believe that?"

She nodded painfully. "Yes, Vivian, because love cheated me. I was the one who thought that love was all-powerful and can do anything. But no, I lost everything, including myself, because of love."

Samaira's memories transported her to another world— the world of Ashish and his mother. Tears welled up in her eyes.

"I believed Ashish and his proclamation of love. I danced with his teddy bears. I trusted his roses. But it was all fake—an illusion. I treasured everything he gave me. I fell for him when he said he would take care of me."

Vivian did not interrupt. She needed to pour out what she had kept bottled inside for a long time.

"We were a popular couple—*jodi*[10] *number one*; our pictures would get plenty of likes. We took thousands of selfies. Everything was perfect outwardly except for my life with him."

---

10 Couple.

Tears rolled down her cheeks. He wiped them gently.

"I gave up my job, Vivian. I made him hot *rotis*. I gave up my world for him . . . all in the name of love, but in the end, he chose another girl with a pretty face despite our marriage."

Vivian tried his best to control the anger that surged within him. He mentally thrashed her ex-husband for treating her the way he did.

"Love did not save me. Love did not protect our relationship. It mocked at me . . . it sniggered at my life. I finally realised that I did not have one anymore . . . no life," she whispered in a dull voice. Swallowing her pain, she continued, "I lost my dreams, I lost myself, Vivian. And you know what this society does?"

He knew all about the harsh realities of life.

"It mocked me for my failure, Vivian. It mocked my inability to hold my husband. Some people even suggested that the girl had something which I did not—"

Vivian put a hand over her mouth. His fingers trembled, and she could see her pain reflected in his eyes. "Enough, Samaira."

She saw his wet eyes. He was crying for her. It melted her inside but strengthened her resolve that he should not be upset because of her.

"Vivian, that is why I fear love. It has ditched me . . . stolen my trust and belief," her voice faltered.

"Samaira, that was not love."

"Everyone said it was love. They told us we made a great pair."

"*Arre*, love is not about everyone; it is about that special someone."

"Playing with words is not going to alter my opinion, Vivian," she said in despair.

Vivian frowned. "Are you an expert, love *guru*?" she mocked.

"I don't claim to be one, but I am not against love."

She looked skeptical. How was he going to convince her? Giving in to his temptation, he moved closer to her. Their faces were inches apart. He tucked the hair on her forehead behind her ears.

"Vivian . . ."

"Listen to me, Samaira. I get what you went through. But you are mature enough to understand that love is not about gifting teddies and roses. It is not about taking selfies together. Love is not about talking for hours."

Holding her hand, he continued, "You are running away, Samaira. You are scared; you are not allowing yourself to feel any emotion, let alone love."

She stared into his eyes.

"Love is the feeling of eternity. I agree that it is a burning sensation that eats you alive, but your heart will long for more. And it is not just about yourself; it is also about your partner. It is the joy of walking together in life, believing that if you fall, your partner will be there for you and hold you forever."

"This is not a competition or debate," protested Samaira.

"Debate or not, it is the truth."

She wanted to deny it, but his argument sounded strong.

"Don't hold yourself back, Samaira. Sometimes life gives you what you desire only when you let go of yourself."

"I don't want to." She was stern.

"Please yourself. I am not here to pressurise you." He rose from his chair.

"Vivian." She caught his hand. "Please don't go," she begged.

"I am not going to be with someone who is determined to be inside their shell. I never thought you were a coward, Samaira," Vivian told her in exasperation.

Seeing her dejected look, he commented, "No one asked you to fall in love. So, I think there is no point in continuing this ridiculous conversation."

She knew that he was upset. "Please don't get me wrong, Vivian. I don't want you to get hurt in the end."

"Why would I?"

"I thought . . ."

"What did you think, Samaira?"

"I had the feeling that you were falling in love with me." Her voice faltered as she gauged his face.

He sighed. He would not put up with this attitude of hers. "Come on, Samaira, did I ever propose to you?"

"No. I mean . . ."

"So, what gave you that idea? And is this your way of warning me off?"

"No, Vivian, please." Her voice trembled.

"You and your weird imagination, Samaira!" he chided.

"But, Vivian, the first time we met, you kissed me. You said to never call you 'bro.'"

"You are a beautiful girl, Samaira. No sane male would want you as a sister except for your own brother."

She blushed a little.

"In the clothing store, when someone addressed me as your wife, you did not correct him," she argued.

"Why should I bother about what other people think? I don't care a damn." His voice was almost harsh.

Almost convinced that she got him wrong, she whispered, "I am sorry, Vivian. I wanted to make sure that you don't—"

She was interrupted rudely. "Get back into your shell. You are safe from me, Samaira. In fact, my girlfriend is coming tomorrow."

She was astonished. She had not expected that.

"Won't your girlfriend get you wrong when she rings you?"

"Are you talking about my caller tune?"

"Yes, I am."

"Kushi admires talent like I do."

Samaira got distracted. "Talent? Don't kid me!"

"What is there to kid? You are an exceptional singer."

"More of a bathroom singer," she repeated Ashish's taunt.

He looked at her as if she was an alien.

"I know my strengths and weaknesses. Yes, I want to sing, but I am not that good. My notes are all over the place. People don't like it."

"If by people you mean your ex-husband or his family, I swear I will thrash him if I ever see him."

"Ha-ha, our friendship blinds you," she replied, nervously.

Vivian pulled her close and shook her hard by her shoulders. "I hope this instils some kind of sense into you."

"Vivian, I spoke the truth."

"Truth? How could you see the truth when you are wearing big blinkers and refuse to take them off?"

"I can't sing."

Feeling as though he was hammering a stonewall, he turned away.

"Vivian, I don't want to lose you."

He scowled. From the moment he entered the restaurant, she had been sending him mixed signals; blowing hot and cold.

"When I came to Bangalore, I began to rebuild my life. I was tied to my past. Without you, I would never have come out of it even the tiniest bit. I want you as my friend. In fact, you are my best friend, Vivian. I don't want to lose you."

Friend-zoned, his mind alerted him. But at least she gave him a chance. Better than *bro-zoned*.

Her melancholic face haunted him. Holding her cheeks, he remarked, "What happened to you, Samaira? You seem intelligent, but somewhere you have lost yourself. Right now, you are floundering like a kid, frightened of everything. People around you will take advantage of that—they will use your weakness. Running away from your life will not help you."

His fingers brushed away her tears. "Life is beautiful. You have to feel it, live it," he paused, observing her. She was breathless as he came closer. Their table was secluded from the crowd.

"Let it go, Samaira, throw away your past. You learned your lessons. It is time to move on."

She listened to his words intently. "Believe in yourself.

Right or wrong, follow whatever your heart says. Even if it guides you wrong, remember . . ."

Her heart thudded in anticipation at what he was about to say. "I will be there to shield your fall . . . to lift you up again." He put his hand on her head and continued, "I promise. You will always have a shoulder to lean on if you make a mistake. After all, life is about making mistakes and learning from them."

"I will try my best," she assured him, taking his hand from her head and holding it tight.

"Together, we can rule."

She nodded in affirmation. Determination glinted in their eyes.

"But only as a friend, Samaira . . . just as you wanted," he agreed finally.

She did not acknowledge that. He withdrew his hand from hers. She wanted to reclaim it. But she was the one who had put in that boundary, and she had to get used to it.

"That is what you want, right? A life without love?"

Her enthusiasm fled, but her decision was made.

"You are right, Vivian. I don't want love . . . only friendship."

"Okay, then. Hope you don't change your mind. Or else, Kushi might get a bit possessive."

"I understand." She bent her head.

He gave her a peculiar look. "Don't worry. I will take care of the bill," he added.

"Vivian," she called out to him as he reached the shop's entrance.

"Yes." He turned to her.

"Thanks for your support."

"I don't want your gratitude, Samaira. What are friends for?"

He walked away, leaving her with the feeling that she missed something important in her life.

CHAPTER SIX

THE DENIED FEELING

∾

Like Navdurga, love takes avatars . . . and the finest
avatar of love is friendship, which glues you with
another for eternity.

Work was hectic. The week began as if nothing
had happened between them. Vivian and Samaira
did not let their weekend meeting get in the
way of their work rapport. She understood why
this campaign was important to him. Five big
corporate organisations were waiting to sign up
with CT based on the success of this one. Their
campaign was being tracked hourly and daily by
their competitors and the corporates to see how
they were going to pull this off successfully.

Samaira put down her pencil and flexed her
arms by stretching them. A small display panel
caught her eye. Someone from the facility team
had placed it near her desk that Monday on
Vivian's order.

"Day one, or one day? You decide."

Without even asking him, she knew that the bold letters were Vivian's. Each day the quotes changed, and she had no idea when he wrote them. She just knew one thing—that they made her bubble with happiness. He was an endearing friend who kept his promise to her. His strategy worked. Reading the quotes motivated her and made her smile.

She collected her papers and entered Vivian's cabin to discuss her latest idea and its implementation. She had invested all her energy in this campaign . . . for CT . . . for Vivian.

"Hello, Vivian." She entered his room with a gentle knock.

"Hey, good morning, Samaira, come in," he welcomed.

"Seems like my boss is in a good mood today," she teased, breaking her inhibitions gradually. It was a good sign.

"Yes. We are doing well with the clothing-store campaign."

"You breathe work, boss," admired Samaira.

He took out a small box from his table drawer and gave it to her.

She was astonished. "What is this?"

"Did you know that curiosity killed the cat?"

She pouted. The box was wrapped in glitter paper with a bow on the top. She ripped off the paper eagerly.

"Hey! Slow down!

That took me at least two minutes to wrap," he complained.

Ignoring him, she took the item out of the box. It was

made of crystal and depicted two thumbs opposite each other wishing good luck. The craftsmanship was exquisite.

"Wow, it is beautiful, but it is broken," she said, dejected. She pointed to a little dent on either side of the thumbs.

"Hah, is it visible? Because I asked him to take it out."

"Take out what? Why did you do that?"

He opened the small drawer again. There was a red heart-shaped crystal.

"This goes on top of those thumbs," he said to her.

"So, you—"

"Yes, you want only friendship, right? And I don't want you to get me wrong," he elucidated.

She nodded. Vivian was honouring her request. She should have felt happy, but strangely she was disappointed. Her good mood shattered into pieces.

Raghu came in. "Vivian, I have mapped Kushi to the digital marketing for Spicy Foods."

"Good. The manager is Mr Ravi, right?"

"Yeah."

"That is great. She will learn from him but warn him to be strict with her. No nepotism at CT," he instructed. His secretary nodded.

"Ring Mr Vadra on the pending payment," he threw out the next order.

"Aye, aye, captain." Raghu marched off with a salute.

"Vivian, when is Kushi arriving? You told me that she will be here this week? Is she going to work here?" Samaira bombarded Vivian with questions.

"It seems like you are more interested in her visit than I am," commented Vivian with a dry smile.

"Not really . . . I am just curious."

"Really, Samaira?" His face portrayed incredulity.

"About my best friend's girlfriend," she retorted.

"Hmm, don't worry. Kushi is one of the sweetest people I have ever known. She is doing her MBA and is coming here as an intern to complete her final year project," he elaborated.

"How does she look?" The question came out of Samaira involuntarily.

"Why does that matter to you?" Vivian's eyes were sharp.

"Vivian, she is your girlfriend and probably your fiancée-to-be. I want to know more about her."

"My fiancée? I wouldn't call her that—at least not yet. But looks-wise, Kushi is beautiful . . . her eyes and long hair would make any man go crazy," sighed Vivian.

She was supposed to be pleased for her friend, but she felt deflated. Her reverie broke with Vivian's words. "Anyway, back to work. Let us see what you have come up with."

She handed over the papers.

***

Kushi was an extremely pretty girl. She fit exactly into the tall-fair-thin category—the most coveted by girls. No one could fault her behaviour. She was sweet, polite, and talented. Reluctantly, Samaira had to acknowledge that she would be the ideal fit for Vivian, who was perfection personified. Ready to make a mountain out of a molehill, she was still not able to find a single flaw in her.

A week went by. To Samaira, Vivian appeared to spend all his time with Kushi. They even went to lunch together. People accepted them as a couple gracefully. Even if someone did not, no one would have dared to raise eyebrows against Vivian.

She approached his office. The door was partly open. The sound of laughter stopped her. She peered through the gap. Vivian and Kushi sat together on the visitors' sofa. Their heads almost touched, and they were going through a file together.

"That is an awesome suggestion, Kushi," applauded Vivian, closing the file.

"Really, Viv? It means a lot to me."

She hugged him exuberantly and kissed him on his cheeks.

"Calm down, teddy bear," he coaxed her as he got up.

"I am one hundred per cent positive that this will work."

"So how much will I get for this brilliant idea?" she asked, following Vivian.

"The company doesn't pay interns, teddy bear," he mocked.

"Hmm, so sad." She pouted her lips.

"I think I will pay from my own pocket if your idea works out . . . maybe my entire salary," he exaggerated. Her eyes gleamed.

"Hah, I am so in love with you, Viv," she declared emphatically.

Vivian ruffled her hair. "I know all about your love, Kushi, but don't take advantage of my name here, at work."

Samaira's world crumbled down around her. It was

obvious that Vivian and Kushi loved each other. The green monster of envy tugged at her, and she couldn't bear to look at them anymore.

Vivian saw her through the opening as she was about to leave.

"Samaira, why are you waiting outside?"

Caught red-handed, she composed herself to meet Vivian.

"Hello, Samaira." Kushi waved at her cheerily. Samaira acknowledged her.

"I will leave now, Viv. I will pass this to my manager," Kushi told him, indicating her file.

"Yes, please, but it is your manager who will be taking the final call, not me," said Vivian.

"The sunshine of the family," he remarked after Kushi left the place.

"The advantage of being young," stressed Samaira. She wanted to tell him that she was too young for him.

"Too young at twenty-two?"

Too young for your twenty-eight, and you are mad.

She wanted to scream those words at him, but she did not.

She talked business instead. "I have come up with the target audience for the clothing store's digital marketing campaign."

Vivian looked at the clock. It was 1.00 p.m.

"*Wah*[11], Samaira, I am almost drained. Let us look at your list after lunch," he told her.

---

11   Used typically to express admiration.

Samaira gave him a curt nod. "Should I call Kushi back?"

"Why?" he inquired, looking confused.

"Your lunch companion, boss."

"Hah, but she is going to lunch with her manager today."

"Oh, I did not know."

"So why don't you join me for lunch? Let us go to the salad corner nearby," he suggested.

"No, Vivian, we can't. I brought my lunch," she responded in a harsh tone.

"Come on, Samaira, ditch your hostel food," he commanded lazily.

"I will not," she retorted.

They looked at each other like two opponents on a war field.

"You are too busy, Vivian."

"I was the one who asked you. If I was busy, why would I invite you for lunch?"

"No, you are . . . you did not even change the quote today," she criticised.

"Hah, caught you; that is the reason my dearest friend is angry with me," he told her playfully.

Samaira lost her cool. "No, Vivian, it is not just that. I refuse to be a replacement for anyone, and certainly not for Kushi."

With that final note, she shut the door, leaving Vivian in his room.

***

It was Friday. She did not speak with Vivian after that encounter. If he wanted Kushi, she could not do a damn thing about it. Her brain assured her heart that it would not torture her with that fact.

"Let it go" was the quotation for that day, and she willed herself to do just that. She was looking at a gloomy weekend ahead. She might take one or two files back to her hostel. She set a reminder on her mobile phone to email those files to herself before the end of the day. That was the only way to keep her mind occupied. A small window popped up on her laptop screen. A new e-mail from the HR team with the subject line "Surprise Party". She opened the e-mail.

Dear employees,

All work and no play make Jack a dull boy and Jill a dull girl.

At CT, we believe that, and we want you to have some fun. So, shut your laptops at 4:59 p.m. sharp and join us at the entertainment hall today @ 5 in the evening. Show off your talents, play games, and win exciting prizes. Groove to the music. Please don't miss it! Be prepared for the thrilling surprises.

Regards,
CT HR Team

This was probably what she needed now . . . some harmless fun instead of moping about Vivian all the time. Her communicator popped up with a group chat.

Preeti: Sami, it is time . . . our stomachs are rumbling . . . join us for lunch.

Shreya: And Preeti's mom has made fish curry today.

Praveen: If you are late, I will finish the fish curry—beware :P

Samaira laughed at that. These people were a part of the new world she had created for herself. Locking her laptop, she took her lunch bag to the cafeteria.

***

"Shreya, we are lucky to have the boss's best friend as our best friend, right?" Preeti tagged Shreya for support. Pulling Samaira's leg was their favourite pastime.

"Is it only friendship?" Shreya pondered.

"We know Sami. How close you are . . . five years in this company and I have not seen him except at the company celebrations and events," sighed Praveen.

"Why don't you introduce us all?" Preeti enthused.

"Let me remind you all. He is a human dynamo, and he knows who is working where."

"All five thousand employees—you got to be kidding," mused Shreya.

"I am not sure. But the moment I mentioned your names, he told me that he knew you all."

"Hah, might be he remembers us because of you." Praveen winked at her.

Normally, she would have playfully dodged their teasing, but her fight with Vivian had made her sensitive.

"He has a new friend now. In fact, a special one," she informed them in a dry tone.

"A special one? A girlfriend?" whispered Preeti.

Samaira nodded grimly.

"Good for him . . . I am looking for one but not able to find her because I am stuck with dumb friends like you." Praveen laughed. Preeti kicked him under the table.

"No fish curry for you," she teased him and dragged the container away from him.

"And, Samaira, since you are new, we have to tell you— don't miss this celebration on any account. It will be full of fun . . . *mast*," advised Shreya.

***

CHAPTER SEVEN

THAT LITTLE PUSH

Just as an eagle needs a push to soar into the sky . . . she needs a gentle nudge to achieve her dreams. And if she falls, he will be there to catch her, lift her, and push her again until she flies to the stars.

Except for courteous wishes and official talk, Vivian had not spoken to her. She had to admit that his ice-cold attitude killed her. No matter what happened between them, the quotes changed daily. That kept her hopes up . . . perhaps they might resolve their differences some day. She fingered the crystal thumbs unconsciously.

When did she begin to classify him as her exclusive property? It was the crux of the issue. She was in the wrong, and she would make the first move. Vivian breezed past her without a second glance, tagging along with Kushi. That hurt her. She looked at the time. It was five in the evening. Shutting her laptop, she went to the entertainment hall.

The cheerful noise hugged her. It was a long time since she had felt that electric atmosphere, and she was thrilled to be back in circulation. The hall had a big auditorium with a huge dais. It appeared as though all the thousand employees who worked at the Bangalore CT office were seated inside. Preeti and Shreya waved at her from the first row. How did they manage to occupy the first row, competing with this crowd? Thanking her friends from her heart, she rushed to them, leaving her troubles and worries aside.

"Hey, people, you are excellent. You got the cream of the seats for us," she appreciated them.

"All credit goes to me," Praveen smirked.

"How modest," condemned Preeti. The voice from the nearby speakers interrupted their conversation.

"Attention, everyone. I am Dinesh, and I am your host for today! Ready to rock?" he roared from the stage. The crowd acknowledged as they yelled back.

"Back to college days," murmured Shreya into Samaira's ears, but she was not listening. Her eyes were riveted on one person, who dominated the stage though he sat with the VIPs of CT.

Vivian. Their eyes clashed. Enough was enough. She would break the ice today. From her seat, Samaira whispered, "Sorry, Vivian. Please don't do this to me."

His eyes were sharp. As if he heard those words, he smiled at her.

"So, let us welcome our young and dynamic CEO to

kick off this event with his peppy talk," the compere invited him. A huge cheer welcomed him as he took the mic.

"Thank you, friends. Without you, CT is nothing, and I thank you all for your hard work and dedication. I am really proud of you . . . love you all."

The crowd whistled and revealed the affection they had for their boss.

"But today is the day to take your mind off work. Enjoy and have fun to the maximum. Thank you."

He returned to his seat. His professional duty was done. The presenter organised a game of Housie for the employees, and prizes were distributed for first/second/ third rows and full house.

Mother luck has deserted me as usual, thought Samaira. She had only four numbers punched when the game finished. But her friend Preeti bagged the full house.

"Congrats!" they screamed. Vivian presented the gift to Preeti, congratulating her. He was about to return the mic to the presenter of the event, who said,

"Not so fast, Mr CEO."

"Our next event, Talent Zone, begins with you."

Vivian lifted both his hands as if in surrender. Dinesh laughed at the gesture.

"Don't worry; it is no big deal. Creative Tanks is about to bring out the hidden talents of their employees . . . let us see what you have. So, what will you do for us? Dance . . . sing?"

"Dancing and singing. I think I will do that in the end, but now I can kick-start the event with a poem of mine."

"Poem . . . wow, Vivian. We never thought you had that

in you. But on one condition—we will suggest a topic for you."

"Okay, so you are not going to make it easy for me today," he sighed.

"Yes, the poem must be on love. After all, you are the most eligible bachelor in the crowd. Girls, make some noise for the CEO!"

Everybody shouted. Vivian closed his eyes.

Love . . .
She ripped my heart and gripped my soul . . .
Her thoughts dripped into me . . .
And now nothing matters anymore . . .
Her dreams are mine, mine are hers . . .
Together, we will walk in the lane of life,
Slowly but steadily towards the sky of success . . .

There was tremendous applause as he gave the mic back.

"Wow, Vivian! Seems like you are bitten by the lovebug," the compere pulled his leg.

He shrugged in response. "I am curious, Vivian. You have to share your secret."

"You will know about it soon." He laughed.

"People, I tried my best," the organiser informed the crowd.

Samaira's heart ached. Kushi was the lucky one. She had misinterpreted all his actions towards her as love. On top of it, she had warned him not to fall in love with her. She blamed herself for her foolishness. How could she be so stupid? Her mind drifted to the incident at the café. He was probably laughing at her argument over love. She sighed.

"Now it is time for the others to play this one . . ."

The event organiser brought out a big box of lots, holding the names of all the employees. Many people came on to the stage. Some were introverts and shy when their names were called out, but some were sportive. They danced to peppy tunes, sang cheerfully, and even enacted skits. Happily, they left the dais with their gift boxes.

"CT guys are really talented," the compere complimented in between.

"Now for the next lot. It is none other than Kushi Vastav."

Her gang of friends cheered for her enthusiastically.

"So, Kushi, what will you do for us? Or, let me ask the crowd here—what shall we ask this pretty lady to do today?"

"Dance! Dance!" some people shouted from the back.

"Viewers' request, Kushi. Dance." The presenter smiled at her.

"I am ready to dance. But I need a partner." Kushi pouted.

"A good request. You can choose your partner . . . after all, it is your dance, and the stage is all yours."

Kushi tied her heart-patterned *dupatta*[12] around her white cotton *salwar* with a knot. She walked over to Vivian

---

12 A length of material worn arranged in two folds over the chest and thrown back around the shoulders, typically with a *salwar kameez*, by women from South Asia.

and held out her hand to him, inviting him to join her for the dance. He put his hands in hers.

"I can't run away from you, teddy bear." He laughed. The crowd whistled. Vivian's white T-shirt and black jeans complemented Kushi's *salwar*.

Tum paas aaye . . .

The DJ played the all-time famous Bollywood song. Samaira closed her eyes and willed them to disappear. It was pure torture to sit and watch them romancing.

How could you, Vivian? But she knew she had herself to blame. She had nipped their relationship in the bud. Had it been a relationship at all? It had started the same way with Ashish, all glitz and glamour, and see how it had ended! She did not want the same to happen between herself and Vivian. And her heart reminded her that Vivian and Ashish were not the same. But Vivian had strong feelings for Kushi, didn't he? How could he love her, then?

Samaira tortured herself with these thoughts, unable to take her eyes off the stage. Vivian held Kushi's hips, and they circled together to the romantic tune. Their bodies swayed gracefully to the rhythm. The crowd went crazy seeing their CEO dance with a girl. The music stopped, and to Samaira it appeared as though they were reluctant to let go of each other.

"Is she the girlfriend you talked about?" murmured Shreya.

Samaira nodded.

"Thanks, Kushi and Vivian. That was an awesome

performance," the organiser commented, bringing back the box of chits. Vivian handed the gift to Kushi.

"Now for the next lucky lot. It is Samaira Ranjan!"

Samaira panicked. She had never expected her name to come out of the thousand names in the auditorium. She wanted to bury herself in her seat.

"Come on, Sami, you are the lucky one," Praveen pushed her to the stage.

"Here comes one of the exceptionally talented new faces in the company," welcomed the organiser from the HR team.

It was a long time since she had performed on stage. There was a time when she had volunteered to conduct these competitions with enthusiasm and had participated in all their college youth festivals. But now everything around her seemed scary. That dimension of her life had changed, and she was not as exuberant as before. With a thudding heart, she went to the dais.

"Ms Samaira Ranjan, what will you perform? Dance or song?"

"I will . . ." she faltered. She was unaware of how pretty she looked in her yellow *salwar* with an embroidered collar. Her green *dupatta* fluttered at her left shoulder.

Vivian joined Dinesh. "I think Samaira will sing. She is my most favourite singer," he announced. That declaration was enough to arouse the audience's curiosity.

"Hah, you have touched the chord of music in Vivian's heart; you must be a special singer." The HR man winked at her. She felt bulldozed by Vivian. She had thought she would make a few dance moves and get off the stage gracefully. But singing? Had he gone mad? She stared at him furiously. Music was her passion. She loved singing, but she had restrained herself after those mean comments from Ashish and his mom.

Before she could say no, Dinesh announced to the crowd.

"Ladies and gentlemen, here we go . . . music for you all. Please get ready to listen to our CEO's favourite singer."

He put the mic in her hands with a smile. Vivian moved to the other side of the dais.

Samaira's hands became cold and clammy. She did not have the guts to look at Vivian as nervousness tied her tongue. She wanted to slap him hard. To her, he deserved it for putting her in this position. Her forehead was covered with beads of sweat. Brushing the drops away, she tried to calm herself. Her hands shivered as she fiddled with the mic. Swallowing the lump that threatened to choke her throat, she attempted to hum the tune of a Bollywood song— *"Taal se . . ."*

Neither words nor music came out. Her memories took her to a place where she did not want to be. Ashish and his mother leered at her.

"Thinks she is a super singer," "More of a bathroom singer," "Good-for-nothing," "Her tone is raw, and her rhythm is completely out of place. Had my music teacher heard her singing, she would have slapped her . . ."

The words taunted her out of nowhere.

She could not sing. She could never . . . what if the entire crowd criticised her like Ashish's mother? What if they puked or ended up with indigestion after her song? Just like Ashish and his mother claimed . . .

She could never do that to her music. Fear overwhelmed her. Her mind went blank. Unconsciousness took over her, and she fainted on the stage.

The crowd gasped.

"What happened?" they inquired.

Vivian rushed to her. "Can someone bring some water?" Bending down, he shook her gently. "Samaira, are you all right?"

Her palms and forehead were wet. He gently dragged her from the stage to the corner.

"A typical case of stage fright," remarked Dinesh as he joined them.

"Not as simple as that, Dinesh. She was the union secretary of her college. This is not a case of stage fright," supported Vivian.

Dinesh was dumbstruck. "Oh."

"You continue with the event, Dinesh. This incident must not disturb the occasion today." Vivian's voice was firm.

A member from the HR team rushed to them with a water bottle.

Vivian sprinkled water on her face. Cradling her head, he whispered, "Samaira, are you all right?"

Droplets of water revived Samaira's consciousness, and her eyes fluttered open.

"Does she need medical attention?" An ERT member came forward.

"Not now, Guna. I can take care. Please give her some space," he told the people, realising that a small crowd was gathering around them. At the CEO's order, they dispersed with reluctance.

"Are you feeling better now?" he murmured in her ears. Still in Vivian's hold, she got up holding his hands. Her legs felt wobbly. Silence captured them. A wave of embarrassment swept through her as she recollected why she fainted. She could not look into his eyes. Guilt overtook her. She had failed him miserably.

"Yes. Thanks for your help," she muttered and moved away from him and the prying eyes of the crowd. The moment she was away from their sight, she ran like mad to the relaxing zone of CT. The area had multiple tables and chairs underneath the lush green trees for the employees to relax and have a cup of coffee. It was virtually deserted, as all the employees were in the entertainment hall.

It was 7.30 p.m. The sun had gone down, and darkness swept the place, except for a few lights here and there. The crescent moon did not help much either, partly hidden behind the clouds. Taking a seat at the extreme corner, Samaira covered her face with her hands, ashamed of herself.

Why did all the bad things have to happen only to her?

Tears rolled down her cheeks.

"Don't cry, Samaira."

She looked at him, directing all her anger towards him. Vivian sat next to her on the chair.

"Are you happy now, Vivian?"

"No." His voice was sincere.

"What? Not satisfied with your revenge?"

"Revenge?" He was perplexed.

Samaira lost herself. She grabbed his white T-shirt and pulled him closer by his collar.

"Don't play your game with me, Vivian. We fought, and you could not handle it; so, you did this. How could you?"

He held her hands tightly and demanded, "How could I? How could I what? How could I make you sing? Is that the sin I committed? I thought you were my best friend," whimpered Samaira.

"Yes, I was, and I still am. I always will be," he declared.

"This is not what a friend does," she criticised and got up.

"What am I supposed to do? Watch you build an invisible wall around yourself? Do you want me to stand by and see you sink into the sea of misery? That is not what a friend does!"

She gasped as she understood what he implied. "Pulling my name from the box was not a fluke, right?"

Vivian's face reddened a little.

"Oh my God! How did I ever trust you?" she wailed.

"Stop it, Samaira. One more word and I will walk out forever," threatened Vivian.

"No, you will not," she told him dully.

"Yes, you are right; I will not," he agreed with a hesitant smile.

"How will I face everyone again? I feel ashamed. I will be the laughing stock of the company." She wept miserably.

"Please don't cry, Sami."

Vivian stood up and hugged her, lending his support. Gently, he ruffled her hair as her sobs subsided into slow hiccups.

"I am sorry," she whispered.

"For what?"

"For throwing mud on you. I did not mean it . . . and for letting you down, Viv. You let the world know that I was your favourite singer and I . . ." Her lips trembled.

"Calm down. Relax."

"Nothing earth-shattering has happened now." He released her from his hold but still stood close. She laughed nervously, communicating indirectly that she did not believe his words.

"I was not ready for it, Vivian."

"You were ready for it years ago, Sami."

She frowned, wondering what he was getting at.

"I tried to provide you with an opportunity for which you fought three years back"

She strained to remember what he was talking about.

"You badly wanted to sing in the youth competition, representing your college, right? But nepotism played, and Anu snatched the chance from you right under your nose."

"How did you know?" she demanded.

"I will tell you, but you tell me." Vivian paused, as if he was exasperated with her. "Where has that Samaira gone?" he continued.

The question shocked her. She herself asked the same question.

"Samaira Ranjan, the outgoing student secretary . . . the rebel for a good cause . . . the one who stood for her friends boldly, not worried about the consequences."

"Who told you?"

"Do you know where Anu works?"

Realisation dawned on her. "At CT?"

"Yes, on the second floor. Anu joined here as a fresher.

She was with my team for four months. I know her profile well. I connected the same college name and the year in your résumé with hers. The moment I heard you sing when I was in the trial room, I dug deeper. And I met her."

She was stunned.

"Anu gave good feedback on me . . . we used to fight a lot earlier," revealed Samaira.

"Look, Sami, it doesn't matter what Anu thinks about you or the crowd sitting over there thinks about you. What really matters is what you think about yourself."

"I think that I am a bad singer, Vivian."

"Is that what you thought ever since you learned singing from the age of five?"

"Learning the notes doesn't make one a good singer," she denied.

"Agreed, but what about the ability to make other people forget themselves when they hear you sing?"

She widened her eyes in disbelief.

"True, Samaira. I forgot myself when you sang on that day."

"But Ashish told me . . ." she stopped herself, holding her hands over her mouth.

"Well, now comes the real reason," he mocked.

"Nothing to mock about, Vivian. What he said was true."

"What did that idiot say?"

"He and his mother told me that they will throw up if they heard me sing . . . and that I would end up in hell if I torture them in the name of music," she reminisced with hurt.

"Just because two mindless, jealous fools told you something, you believed them? Did you not believe what your 'guru' told you?"

"You spoke with Lakshmi Auntie?"

"Yes, Sami, before I pushed you onto the stage, I did my homework well."

"Obviously, Anu would have told you; both of us were trained by the same teacher."

"Forget it. What did your tutor tell you when you stopped going to her classes after your engagement?"

She closed her eyes. Lakshmi Auntie's words echoed within her.

"Music is within your soul, Samaira; don't stop singing on any account. One day I want to see you as a successful singer, and I will shout to the world that I was your teacher."

"Remember those words, Sami?" taunted Vivian. Her eyes clouded with tears.

"I think you have been robbed in the name of love by two unscrupulous people; they have taken your life, broken your wall of confidence, destroyed the flower of hope, and dashed your dreams."

Vivian's words penetrated her mind.

"You offered them so much power over you . . . you handed them the key to your happiness."

Her body shivered as Vivian hit her with blocks of truth.

"And the worst part is, you are still letting them manipulate you . . . your past dominates you."

He came closer and touched her wet eyelashes.

"Don't waste your tears what does not matter anymore. Open your eyes to the present, Sami. Let the past go."

He brushed his lips against her eyes. His voice mesmerised her.

"Let the real Samaira come out."

His hands held her hips, and his lips whispered against her face. "Please."

His gentle voice did wonders to her wounded soul. She had lost her dreams and passion to someone. She too longed to be as she was before—the bubbly, and easy-going Samaira, instead of the bitter Samaira who was fed up with life.

"I will try."

"Good, and I will be there for you."

His intense look kept her captive. Their clothes fluttered in the gentle breeze. The moon peeped from behind the clouds. Holding hands, they were spellbound. Time stood still. Mesmerised by the moment, Samaira leaned towards him. He did not avert his glance for a second. They were caught in the moment, created especially by Cupid.

Vivian's mobile phone rang, shattering the spell.

"Damn, I swear that I will throw away my mobile someday," he cursed.

The moment was gone. The spell broke. "Oh my!" She blushed.

Vivian attended the call. "Yeah, she is all right; no need for a doctor now . . . yes, I will be there."

"The HR representative called me. The event is about to end . . . I have to go."

She smiled. "Yes, I understood that, boss. Let me lead you this time," she volunteered playfully.

As Vivian walked behind her, Samaira promised herself,

I will make you feel proud of me just like how you make me feel proud of you . . .

CHAPTER EIGHT

THE COMEBACK

Hold my hands and I know I will climb to the top. If I crash, you will be there to break my fall. And I will climb again, holding your hands as before . . .

Samaira ran back to the entertainment hall leaving a puzzled Vivian behind. His pace was fast, but she was agile like a rabbit.

What is she up to?

The craziness in her leapt out, and he was glad of that change. The event was about to end. He had to deliver a formal vote of thanks, and then there would be dance and dinner to close the session. A big surprise awaited him as he went back.

"I am back . . . Samaira Ranjan," she was saying. The crowd booed, and she understood that it would be difficult to get their attention. But it was worth a try for the sake of her best friend. Is that all he was? She did not have time to speculate on that.

Vivian was astonished to hear her soft-spoken voice, which reverberated around the hall through the speakers. "Hey, I never knew that you people are more powerful than chloroform."

Now she had their attention. "One look at you all and I fainted. Come on, cheer me up; I entertained you one way or the other."

She connected with them with her humour, and they responded with laughter. Vivian smiled, and he went back to the corner of the stage. He would not miss a second of her action.

"Now I am back to entertain you, and please don't worry; I am not about to faint again. This time I swear I will entertain you in another way. How about a song—a song from our boss's favourite singer?"

The audience cheered her on with their applause.

She took a deep breath and cleared her throat. Deliberately, she cleared her mind. She blocked all the external factors cluttering her thoughts; she would deal with them later. She would get the verdict on her musical talent from the audience, not from Ashish or his mother.

The initial background score soothed her nerves. Her soul went into a world where musical notes lived. Stealing a few, she brought them to her throat. The lyrics came to life.

Tu safar mera
Hai tu hi meri manzil
Tere bina guzara
Ae dil hai mushkil . . .

The hypnotic song reverberated all over the hall. The crowd became silent, hooked to her voice. The babies in the crowd stopped crying. People paused whatever they were doing as their hearts voyaged with the soul-shattering tune of Amitabh Bhattacharya's song.

She made them feel the emotions behind it, and they lived the song for the two minutes she sang. The music tantalised them, and they were with her through every note. They listened to her voice, spellbound. A few had tears in their eyes and sat motionless; she had made that connection with the audience. Her song was perfect.

After her performance, she slowly opened her eyes and observed the audience to gauge their reaction with a thudding heart. The silence taunted her more than their booing.

Was Ashish right after all? Seconds ticked by, and her heartbeats became erratic.

The doubts crept back into her mind. Then, the applause broke out to become thunderous, and the men at the back whistled. They kept cheering and did not want to stop. The electrifying response made her glance coyly at Vivian. She almost choked with happiness to see him applauding, exactly like the crowd. He winked at her.

"Thanks," she murmured her gratitude.

Her husky voice and flawless music had mesmerised

every individual in the crowd. From the stage, Dinesh declared, "Yes, Samaira, truly an amazing performance! The best of the lot. Now we all know why our boss declared you his favourite singer. So how about getting your gift?"

Vivian took the gift from Dinesh and presented it to her.

"Congratulations, Samaira; you did it."

Someone captured that special moment, as a flash of light went by. The event ended with Vivian's vote of thanks. The employees were requested to have dinner, which was arranged at the other end of the hall. The stage was lit with disco lights. The dance floor was ready.

Shreya dragged the gang to the stage. "Come on, people, our dinner is not going to run away. Let us groove to the music and feel the rhythm; it has been a long time since I danced with Vijay."

"You and your one-sided crush," chided Preeti.

"Come on, don't squash my dreams with your brutal words. I was about to ask Vijay to dance with me."

Shreya stuck her tongue out as she went in search of Vijay. Samaira joined her friends on the stage. The VJ played light jazz music. She moved to the beats along with Praveen and Preeti. About fifty people enjoyed the music and dance. Except for the colourful lights, the entire area was dark. The VJ changed the dance mood; he switched to a romantic song. Preeti and Praveen turned to each other. They almost forgot Samaira and the other employees around them.

How did she miss this? Preeti and Praveen had feelings for each other. Her heart swelled with happiness. Not wanting to intrude, Samaira stepped back into the darkness.

Someone from behind caught her by her hips and

twirled her around. Before she could protest, she found herself gazing into Vivian's twinkling eyes.

"Vivian, you scared me," she complained.

"Who else can touch you except me?" He sounded possessive.

"What do you mean?" she tried to push him.

"It means that we are going to dance. Don't make a big deal out of it," he reassured her, pulling her back into his arms.

"Hmm, you are a persuasive fellow," she admonished.

"Am I?"

"Yes, you are, and I want to thank you," she murmured into his ears.

"Thank me for what?"

"Is this a session of questions and answers? Don't act innocent. You know what I mean."

"If you are talking about your song and the audience's response, the credit is all yours, and I am not going to take it away from you."

Their bodies swayed in unison to the tune. Vivian's hold on her tightened around her hips. She put her hands over his shoulders. Their eyes danced, celebrating her success.

"You pushed me."

"That was nothing."

"If you don't accept my thanks, I will not dance with you," she threatened.

"I don't want your gratitude, Samaira."

Before she could protest, he continued, "Your 'thanks' shoves me away from our relationship. I promised that I will stand for you, and I am just delivering on my promise."

His words confused her.

"But if you want to thank me, you can do it in another way."

"I will do whatever you ask me to do . . . at least today," she promised him.

"That is a 'big' promise; you are putting your foot in your mouth," taunted Vivian.

"I will stand by my words," she reiterated.

"Hmm . . . prove it."

"What do you want me to do?"

With the dance, Vivian had steered them to a secluded corner. They could see people dancing at the other end. He drew Samaira closer so that their bodies touched intimately. Her soft face was plastered against his muscular chest.

She was breathless but could hear his accelerated heartbeat, despite the noise. Passion and romantic music made him whisper, "Kiss me, Samaira."

She turned to him and sensed the longing in his eyes. She was caught like a deer in the hunter's net but did not want to escape. Her eyelids fluttered, and she reacted to his words as if in a trance. She put her hands on either side of his face and pulled him down to meet her trembling lips. Her heart went wild as she made the first move for the first time in her life. She did not stop to think if she was doing the right thing. Their lips brushed, and the only thing that stopped them from taking it further was the fact that they were in a public place, where anyone could see them.

"God, you kept your promise, Sami; you have no idea how much you tempt me," Vivian murmured.

"Let us get back to the crowd or I will not be responsible

for what happens next," he said, with a pulsating desire that vibrated between them.

Samaira blushed, and they walked back to join their friends. After a sumptuous dinner, Vivian dropped her at her hostel. It was ten in the night. As she was about to get off his car, Vivian held her hands tightly. Her eyes met his with a question.

"Stay this way, Samaira; this is the real 'you.' Good night."

His voice echoed in her head, and she saw his car disappear down the road.

***

Productivity improved significantly after the gala event. Samaira became a popular personality at the office. People came over and appreciated her. She felt motivated. She also realised that the relationship she shared with Vivian was not just friendship.

Friendship did not entertain possessiveness. And to her shame, she was horribly jealous of Kushi.

"*Speak of the devil and there she comes*" Samaira's mind bitched.

"Hello, Sami . . . loved your song," Kushi said breezily and walked past her to Vivian's room.

Time ticked by. It was more than half an hour since Kushi had gone in.

What were they doing? Her imagination went riot. Was he holding her hips and kissing her as he had kissed her that day? Or did he push her onto the office sofa and . . .

She could not even bear to imagine Vivian with another girl. She itched to grab her by her *dupatta* and throw her out. She could not wait anymore. With a feeble excuse, she barged in without knocking. He raised his eyebrows, and his forehead lifted a little.

It appeared that Kushi and Vivian were in deep discussion. Her face was clouded in distress. Vivian had his hands on her shoulders as if consoling her.

"Damn you, Vivian . . . you play knight in armour for every damsel in distress," she muttered.

"What is that, Samaira? Anything urgent?"

"I mean . . . no." She shook her head.

"Then, can you please leave? We have something personal to discuss." Vivian caught her eyes, hoping Samaira would not get him wrong.

"I understand you well," her eyes flashed back.

She closed the door noisily in response, in anger. "You test my patience to its limits," she murmured and kicked the door. Two girls who came that way looked at her as if she had lost her senses.

She returned to her desk and calmed herself down before she became mad. What right had she over Vivian to act in this manner? Did she love him? Would she label the feelings she had for him as "love"? She was not sure.

She covered her cheeks with her hands. She was not sure of her feelings, and she had no right to behave in this fashion or to shout at Vivian. The confusion was not going to help her sort out her feelings. He had all the right in this world to find his happiness . . . to look for his soulmate, to discover love.

With her words, she had broken whatever they had between them earlier. Her heart mocked at her own words— "only friendship." She wanted more than that. She was open to explore her feelings and did not mind getting burnt in the process. She was ready. Her shell had broken, and he had created that change in her. But how to convey that to him . . . that she would no longer run away from her feelings?

Kushi's meeting was done. Vivian accompanied her out of the room.

His eyes sought out Samaira. She dropped her eyes back to her laptop. Vivian came over and put his hands on the desk.

"Sami."

She blanked out the irritation to shout at him. "Yes, boss."

"Did you like the quote today?"

It said, "Every day is a new day with a new beginning."

"It is nice . . . pepped me up to start my work with a cup of strong coffee," she said, almost forgetting her anger.

Vivian loved the newer version of Samaira more. Outgoing, vivacious, and confident.

"All you needed was a bit of oil."

"Don't you dare to call me rusty!"

"You should know by now that you should not dare me," he mocked.

Her mind focused back on the problem at hand. "Issue with Kushi?" she asked, hoping that he would elaborate.

"Nothing that I can't handle." He smiled, and Samaira knew that. Vivian could tackle anything. The bond strengthened between them. Sometimes they even communicated without words.

"Why did you barge in, my curious cat?" Vivian winked at her.

"I was not curious."

"Really?" Vivian queried dryly, obviously not believing her.

"I wanted to show you something." She took out a card from her desk.

Dear Samaira,

Thanks for your interest in our program "Top Singer of India." We welcome you to the first level of auditions in Chennai.

Planet TV
Venue: The Mount Theatre
Time: 11.00 a.m.

Vivian applauded her mentally. Planet TV was one of the top channels in India, and Top Singer of India topped the charts according to the TRP reports. The show ran once a year. She had responded to his push. Not everyone in this world capitalised on the encouragement they received.

"Wow, Samaira, I am impressed," he appreciated. "I don't see a date." He turned the card either side to check it out.

"They called up and confirmed the date, Vivian. It is tomorrow. I must leave tonight. That is why I came in to request you for the day off."

"Consider it granted. Anyway, we have almost done our part for the campaign. We have to wait and watch how it goes."

"Yes, I am super excited about it," she enthused. Her interest was evident on her face.

"Sami, have you booked your ticket for tonight's journey?"

"Not yet."

"Don't do that," he commanded.

"But you granted me leave," she complained in disappointment.

"I have to meet the CEO of *Awzome* tomorrow for some discussions on the deal. If they are satisfied with the service they have received so far, we might be able to extend the contract for another year."

"Happy for you, Vivian," she congratulated him.

"Don't count your chickens before they hatch. I will be leaving for Chennai tomorrow, early in the morning. Your program is at two in the afternoon. We can reach there before that. Join me. You go to the auditions. I'll take care of business and we can head back to Bangalore together."

For a moment, Samaira was stunned by his suggestion. Vivian misinterpreted her silence.

"As a friend . . . nothing more . . . nothing less," he assured her.

So, it was his turn to friend-zone her now. She would make him eat his words.

"Yes, nothing more . . . nothing less," she agreed.

You will tell me soon that I am more than a friend, Vivian, and that is a promise.

It was almost five when she shut down her laptop. She had a hectic evening ahead. She had to pack her bag and train her voice. She had to give her best at the audition. She must not let herself—or her Vivian—down.

When did he become hers? She blushed. Her mobile phone rang.

"Are you all done, Sami?" Vivian asked.

"Yes."

"I have some pending work. I will leave late. I called you to confirm that I will pick you from your hostel at five in the morning. Will that be okay with you?" he inquired.

"It would be perfect," she answered.

"And, Sami, enjoy the climb . . . practice well."

"Yes, I will," she promised.

The call disconnected. That evening, she focused on practicing. The car horn beeped exactly at five in the morning at the entrance of her hostel. She rushed out.

"Wow, you look pretty," he told her.

She wore a blue embroidered saree, with a blouse that glittered like gold. Her hair was plaited, but a lock fell on her forehead. She looked traditional with a black *bindi* on her forehead. He looked his suave self, dressed in the cream-colored suit they had purchased at the *Awzome* store.

"A *devi*[13] before me? Or am I still dreaming?" he asked her.

---

13 Goddess.

Samaira pinched his arm hard.

"Ahh, you are cruel," he grumbled.

"You are awake . . . standing in the world of reality; to be precise, driving in the world of reality." She grinned.

"You are a demon, Samaira," Vivian chided her, rubbing his arms.

"Just checking if you will take me safely; I don't want my driver sleeping," she told him haughtily.

Vivian pointed his fingers to himself. "And remember, Vivian, this is what you get for being good to your friend."

"Too modest; come on, let us go."

CHAPTER NINE

INSPIRATION IS ALL AROUND YOU

Surrounding yourself with positive people can be your best inspiration; so can observing a caterpillar transform itself into a butterfly. After all, who could be a greater inspiration than Miss Nature?

Vivian and Samaira were content to be together. They enjoyed the silence for the first ten minutes. "A peaceful time to drive in Bangalore," she observed.

"Hmm, yeah . . . so why are you dressed in a saree?"

"Why do you think?"

"Guessing game, Sami? Probably you want to meet your relatives or a special friend in Chennai?"

Samaira's body tensed. "I don't have anyone."

"Come on, relax! I was pulling your leg," cajoled Vivian.

"I have planned to sing a classical song for the audition . . . hence the saree," she clarified.

"Yes, that makes sense." Vivian nodded.

"I am smart," she declared.

"Seems like when you are into something, you are completely involved," said Vivian.

She yawned, covering her mouth. "That was not graceful." He laughed.

"I was practicing the entire night. I did not get time to sleep," she reasoned.

Samaira dozed off. She did not remember when her eyelids closed. Her face was pressed against Vivian's shoulders, and she had leaned on his chest. Her saree fluttered against his neck. Her shampooed hair enticed him, and he inhaled her fragrance. His attention was distracted by her lovely vision.

Oh hell, this was a different kind of torture.

His lips brushed her hair. Never had a journey been so interesting before. He had purposely left his driver behind. He would not miss a second of the privacy that they got with this trip. He fervently wished that she would realise that the relationship that pulled them together was not merely friendship . . . it was more than that.

She woke up with a start. Her face reddened.

"Oh dear!" She sat up quickly, adjusting her saree. "You should have woken me up," she said, to cover up her embarrassment.

"Why should I?"

What could she reply to that? "I—"

"Don't worry, Sami; I did not mind it. I enjoyed the view," he laughed.

She tapped him on his shoulder.

"You hit me twice today, Sami; beware of the consequences," he threatened her.

"I will compensate for it." She took out two lunch boxes from her handbag.

The fresh smell of *rotis* tempted his nostrils.

"Oh God, I would die for breakfast. I didn't have any as we started early," he said.

"Here comes the solution for your hunger—hot *rotis* and *aloo subzi*[14] for you."

"Did you make it for me?"

"Yes, I got special permission from the warden to use the kitchen." She leaned forward slightly, turning to look at him, and winked.

Vivian wanted to hug her and never let her go. No other girl had taken an interest in his well-being. Most of them were just interested in his pocket.

She opened her box. "Should we stop over to have this?" he asked.

"No . . . I mean it is not safe to park in a corner; it is still dark," she told him.

"But, Sami, I want those *rotis* now. Did you hear that noise? That was my stomach rumbling," he said, patting his stomach.

"I will not deny you your *rotis*; I made it for you, Viv," she told him.

---

14 A potato dish.

She rolled a piece of curry with the *roti* and took it close to his mouth. "Have it. You have been driving for more than an hour now."

Her concern touched him. Her cold fingers touched his lips as she fed him the *roti*. His body shuddered at her touch. "How is it?" She waited for his verdict.

He swallowed it in one go. "Oh my God . . . so good! The roti is too soft . . . aloo is perfect. There's a master chef inside you!"

I hope I feed him many breakfasts in future, she prayed to God fervently.

Temptation overtook Vivian. With each passing second, it was becoming difficult to see her as just a friend. Also, his intuition told him that she wanted more from him. But he did not know when they would get the opportunity to discuss their feelings. He did not want to begin any conversation that would disturb the rapport they had right now.

He had a little *subzi* smeared on the side of his lips. "You eat like a child," she chided him gently. Inching near him, she stretched her arm and wiped it off with her hand. The moment her fingers met his lips, an intense feeling of electricity coursed through them.

She gasped. She pulled her hand back as if her fingers had been burnt.

He reacted quickly and grabbed her hand. With one hand on the steering wheel and the other holding hers, he tasted the *subzi* on her fingers. Her body appeared to be highly charged, and she was sensitive to his touch.

Her eyelids fluttered. Her stomach clenched as he moaned. Her cheeks burned, and even her feet tingled at the chemistry between them. She struggled to meet his eyes. Desire made her blush.

"Yum, this is tastier." His voice was husky.

"Sorry," she blabbered the first thing that came to her mind.

That effectively poured cold water on the feelings burning between them.

"Sorry? You are sorry? Forget it, Samaira."

"But, Vivian." She said, hand reaching out towards his face.

He drew back and moved away. "Let us not discuss this further; I assure you that this will not happen again."

With tears in her eyes, she leaned back against her seat. He was not ready to listen, and she would not waste her time breaking her head against a stone wall. But her emotions were disturbed. She closed her eyes lest he saw the sorrow buried in them.

Vivian glanced at her. He knew that she was crying.

Oh God, he had never meant to hurt her; she had drawn the lines clearly. He was the one who had crossed them.

He thumped his hands against the steering wheel in frustration. The rest of the journey passed in silence. The weather in Chennai was warm and sunny. It was almost nine-thirty in the morning.

"Your audition is at eleven, right?"

"Yes." She nodded.

The time for her audition got closer. As the clock ticked by, a feeling of anxiety gripped her. This was a big move for her. To be honest, she had registered in the competition to show Vivian that she was not a loser.

Sensing her discomfort, Vivian took her hand. It was ice-cold. Had he disturbed her equilibrium in the morning?

"Samaira, are you worried?" he demanded.

"No . . . no," she denied.

All the symptoms were there. Her words came out slurred. Her hands were icy. She twisted her handkerchief nervously, and most of all, she did not meet his eyes.

"Relax, Samaira; if it is about the morning, I give my word that—"

Angrily, she put her hand over his mouth. "Stop it, Viv. I have no regrets about this morning; I was a willing participant. Stop talking like a saint," she spat out.

"Then what is your problem?"

She let out a deep sigh. "I am a bit nervous about the audition," she murmured. Vivian had to strain to hear the words.

"I miss your motivation board today," she added.

Vivian parked the car next to the Refresh Park. It was one of the biggest in the city.

"Won't we miss the audition?" she asked, looking at her watch. It was 9.40 a.m.

"Your venue is only ten minutes away—so don't worry."

"Your meeting?"

"I will take care of it, Samaira."

He stopped the man with the coffee can and got two cups. With steaming coffees in their hands, they went inside and occupied a bench.

"First, you deserve an applause."

"Applause?"

"Yes, you have taken the next step on your own," he told her.

"So now is the time for a pat on the back."

He patted her shoulder appreciatively.

"Vivian, don't treat me like a kid."

"Did I treat you like one in the car?"

"That was different." She blushed.

"When you are appreciated, don't be modest . . . don't deny it. People praise you only when you deserve it."

"Okay, I deserved *that*, but now I am scared. What if I fail? What if everything goes wrong?"

"*Arre* relax, Sami; you will do wonderfully well. I completely trust you."

"That is what scares me the most, Vivian. I don't want to break your trust in me."

Keeping the coffee cups aside, he took her hands in his. "A bit of caffeine should have motivated you," he teased.

"*Wah*, I miss your display board today," she confessed a second time.

"Glad to hear that, but you don't always need a motivational quote to push you."

She did not look convinced. Putting his arm around her shoulders loosely, he urged her to stand up. "Look around you, Sami; whatever you see is an inspiration."

He pointed to the blue sky. "Look up. It tells you to aim higher and higher."

He pointed to the bamboo at the corner. The board underneath it said, "Planted in 2012."

"There was nothing at all here until last year; I have seen

this place before. So, five years have passed but look now . . . ninety feet in just one year. How cool can that get!"

"These bamboos did not give up the will to survive, and the one who planted them did not give up hope." Vivian's words made sense.

"Don't give up, Sami. Be like the bamboo."

Samaira was astonished at how Vivian looked for inspiration in every aspect of nature.

"Look at the gentle and calm lake. What does that tell you? Create ripples wherever you go, Sami . . . just like the lake."

She smiled. Her tension ebbed from her body gradually.

He pointed to a little girl who had a balloon in her hand. She tried to blow it, but instead of blowing air, she kept sucking it. She tried again. They observed her for two minutes. She attempted to blow it up, but her effort ended in vain.

"Should we offer to help her?"

"No." He shook his head.

"She will do it. She has the determination in her eyes. Wait and watch."

His words came true. Finally finding a way to blow, she held the inflated pink balloon in her hands and cried, "Yippee!"

"To see the joy in her eyes is priceless," commented Samaira.

"True; the girl never gave up, Sami. She tried repeatedly, and now she has what she wants. And I want to see the same joy in your eyes when you reach your destination."

She nodded with gratitude in her eyes.

"You are talented, Samaira, and you know that. Don't let the irrational fear of what-ifs overrule you; even if you fail, it does not matter, but don't ever stop trying."

She agreed with a smile.

"Good luck, Sami." He clasped her hands.

"Good luck to you too." She squeezed back.

They walked back to the car, determined, minds focused on their goals.

***

Five hours later, they met again at the beach. Samaira was the first to reach there. She had already messaged him to say that she was waiting for him in front of the lighthouse.

Vivian waved at her. She glanced at him. He had changed his clothes. She concluded that in a casual round-necked black T-shirt and a pair of Bermuda shorts, he looked gorgeous.

She lowered her head, to avoid giving in to the temptation to stare at him like an adolescent. He rushed to her. "What happened, Sami? Did something go wrong with the audition?"

She did not answer. He did not press further. *Let her tell me at her own pace*, he thought. They walked towards the beach. Kids ran here and there. Colourful balloons and kites flew in the sky. The vendors stuck sticks of light in the soft sand. The aroma of hot *bajjis*[15] and *chana*[16] tempted them.

---

15 A spicy Indian snack or entree dish similar to a fritter, with several variants.

16 Chickpeas, especially when roasted and prepared as a snack.

"Are you hungry, Samaira? Did you have anything for lunch?"

Not waiting for her reply, he went to the *bajji* stall and got a plate of potato *bajjis*. The moment he handed over the plate to her, tears welled up in her eyes.

What did he do now? "You've got to tell me, Sami. What is wrong?"

"I miss them," she whispered.

"Your parents?" He knew that she had lost her parents recently in an accident.

"Yes . . . we used to come here every Sunday, and I always fought with my brother for this *bajji*. Had I known that he would never come with me again, I would have given him my entire share."

Her hands trembled, and the chutney splattered down.

"We used to play here, and when I felt low, I came here with my father for a walk; he used to guide me," she turned to him and continued— "just like you."

"Father, Sami? Don't you remember what I did when you called me 'bro'?"

Samaira remembered that moment and coloured with embarrassment as she thought about his kiss. She put her hand on her hip and questioned him, "Don't you think what you did was wrong, Viv?"

He let out a sigh. "Yes, but I really don't know what got into me when you called me 'bro'; I couldn't take it. But when I came back to Bangalore, I felt bad about taking advantage of a girl who was obviously sad, and I wanted to apologise for my behaviour. That day haunted me."

"The kiss or the guilt?" Samaira wanted her pound of flesh.

"Both, I guess, but things changed the moment you stepped in for an interview at CT. With other delicious kisses, the first one took the backstage, though it will always be imprinted in my memory," grinned Vivian.

"I will never forget that moment," she declared but with a hint of pride.

Their eyes were locked, and they were tuned to each other's feelings. *If this is not love, what is?* Samaira's heart probed.

"You did not tell me how your audition went," he complained.

"And you did not tell me what happened to your meeting about extending the deal." She pouted.

Checkmate!

"Okay, close your eyes," he instructed as he opened a message on his mobile phone.

"You too," she ordered him before taking a card out of her handbag.

They exchanged their items with eyes closed.

"Ready . . . one, two, three," they chorused in unison.

Opening his eyes, Vivian read the card.

Dear contestant,

Congratulations! You have cleared the audition. You have passed the voice test and the screen test. Please be ready to take part in the first round of the competition. The date will be intimated soon. Good luck for your forthcoming singing journey.

Regards,
Planet TV

Samaira read the message. It was an SMS from the CEO of *Awzome*.

We are impressed with CT's work on the marketing campaigns for our clothing store. We noticed a significant improvement in sales. We would like to extend our contract for three more years. Please continue with the good work. My team will send the contract soon.

They glanced at each other. "Hurray! You did it!" enthused Vivian.

"You too." She hugged him tight with all her strength.

"Hey, you squeezed me out. Never knew you hide so much strength in your body."

"I am a wonder woman." She patted herself on her shoulders.

"Ha-ha, true ... *my* wonder woman," he declared thickly.

She felt cherished when she was with Vivian.

CHAPTER TEN

VIVIAN'S PAST

Carry only the lessons from the past,
not the past. Holding on to the past
tightly might choke your future;
leave it behind and move on . . .

"This wonder woman is about to build a castle," enthused Samaira.

Vivian frowned.

"Don't sit idle. Don't you know, building is tough work? Help me," she commanded.

"You have become bossy," he criticised.

"Have I?" Samaira laughed and threw some sand playfully on his thighs.

"*Wah*, what happened to you?" Vivian adored her attitude, which spelt innocence.

"Beware . . . the next time, I might aim at your eyes," she warned.

"If this is the real Samaira, I never want her to come out," commented Vivian wryly.

"You are lying. Admit it! You like me more this way." With those words, she dragged him towards her. Laughing, they built the sandcastle together, enjoying the salty sea breeze.

Temptation overtook Samaira, and she called the ice-cream trolley that crossed them.

"*Pista*[17] *kulfi*[18] is delicious here. You must try it . . . at least once in your lifetime," advised Samaira.

"Why should it be only once in a lifetime?"

"Are you planning to come here again?"

"Who knows? My future wife might be a *madarasi*, and she might pester me to visit this beach every week," hinted Vivian.

"Be serious, Viv." She grabbed his hand and hauled him up to choose his flavour of *kulfi*.

She ordered her favourite one—pista.

"The same for me," he told her.

"You don't want to try anything else?"

"I trust your taste." He winked. Before he could get his, she had begun eating hers.

"Oh God, I am so happy after a long time!" she exclaimed.

He ruffled her hair with affection. "Always stay this way," he advised her.

---

17   Pistachio.
18   A type of Indian ice cream, typically served in the shape of a cone.

"I intend to." Spelling out her conviction clearly, she proceeded to enjoy her *kulfi*. Her fair skin gleamed under the sun. Her ear hoops were a perfect match for her saree. She projected the aura of an angel. A gentle breeze embraced them. He wanted this moment to last forever.

Her cheeks and lips had liquefied *kulfi*, and it ran down her chin.

"Sami, you are like a kid," he mocked.

"I *am* a kid."

"Let me check," he taunted and brushed his fingers against her lips. An electric sensation shot through her. His eyes met hers as he saw the yearning reflected in her eyes. She was not immune to him.

"Hmm, no more a kid; you are becoming more of my woman each day," he whispered in her ear. Tracing his fingers on her lips, he wiped the remains of the *kulfi*. Cuddling her he commented, "I bet this will taste far better than mine."

Samaira stood speechless as her veins throbbed. The ache in the pit of her stomach intensified in anticipation, and she knotted his T-shirt nervously. Trembling, she caught his hands and whispered, "No, Viv."

She swallowed uncertainly. Ignoring her, he sucked his finger, which had her *kulfi*. Relishing the taste, he commented, "Yum, I was right; this is divine . . . nectar."

"Stop it, Viv." She blushed.

"*Arre*, Sami, nothing to get embarrassed about. This was bound to happen sometime," he proclaimed with a wink. Mortified, she ran away. But he caught up with her soon.

They explored the beach, collected shells, and had *pani puris*[19] to their hearts' fill. They travelled back to Bangalore with delightful memories.

They realised finally that God had made them for each other. But they never spoke the three magic words. Vivian knew that Samaira had changed her perception of love.

She got off at her hostel.

"That was a lovely trip, Viv. Thanks," she said.

"It was a pleasure travelling with you," he replied.

"Okay, then." She was about to leave.

"Sami, I have arranged a surprise anniversary celebration for my parents this Saturday evening. Will you join us, please?"

"At your home?"

"Yes."

"I will be there," she assured him.

***

Saturday arrived. She was all excited as she got ready to go to Vivian's house. He had always kept his business and family separate. He did not even speak about his family much. His background was pretty much a mystery to all his employees.

---

19 A common street snack in several regions of the Indian subcontinent. It consists of a round, hollow *puri* (a small, round piece of bread made of unleavened wheat flour and deep-fried)—fried crisp and filled with a mixture of flavored water (commonly known as *imli pani*), tamarind chutney, chilli, chaat masala, potato, onion, or chickpeas.

But Vivian had invited her home. She twirled around in the room in delight. To him, she must be special, or she would not have gotten that invite. Just being with Vivian made each day exhilarating. Not a day went without their funny banter or silly fights. The Chennai trip proved to be the turning point in their relationship. Kushi went out often, and she spent little time with Vivian that week. To Samaira, it was a good sign. She went out for lunch and dinner with him, and he dropped her at the hostel each night. She felt safe and secure with him . . . just as she had with her father.

That brought a smile on her lips. It was a compliment, but he didn't see it that way. His apartment was a stone's throw from the office and close to the hostel. She rang the doorbell exactly at five. She had arrived half an hour early, but she had to pass through rigorous security and the reason for her visit.

Vivian's mother answered the door.

"Hello, Auntie," she murmured, a little taken aback. She had expected Vivian, not his mother.

"Hello." Vivian's mother waited for her to elaborate further. With a chubby round face and curly hair, she did not resemble Vivian at all. She wore a pink cotton saree. Did he take after his father then? Her mind yearned to collect every small titbit of his life.

"I am here to meet Viv . . . the boss," she amended.

Mrs Andhera frowned. The girl wore a floral-patterned full-length gown with a white lace overcoat. Though she looked pretty with her ponytail and diamond studs, it was not exactly official attire. Never had Vivian invited anyone from office home. He kept his work at the workplace.

"Is he expecting you?" she inquired.

Samaira was miffed. If he had invited her, he should have at least informed his mother about it.

"Samaira, is that you?" Vivian strolled towards them.

He looked young in his pyjamas. The stern look he usually wore like a second skin at the office was gone, and her heart went out to him.

"Ah . . . then you are expecting her." Vivian's mother said. "Come in . . . Samaira, right?"

"Yes." Samaira nodded, a little unsure of her welcome. Vivian's father joined them wearing an ethnic blue kurta.

"Any friend of Vivian's is a friend of mine. Please don't mind us. Today is our wedding day, and we are about to leave for the temple now," she told Samaira, noting the uncertainty in her eyes.

"Okay," muttered Samaira, embarrassed.

"Probably Kushi will be back before us," Mr Andhera told his wife.

"Yes, but please stay, Samaira; we shall have dinner together," she commanded gently, underlining her hospitality.

"Auntie, I don't want to be any trouble," she protested.

"No trouble at all. Pavi!" she called. The maid rushed to her and she gave her instructions.

Samaira caught the word "*roti*" and it triggered another memory. She looked at Vivian. He winked. Their wavelengths matched, and it slowly dawned on her that Vivian was her soulmate. Ashish and his derisions faded away, into the background. Vivian permanently occupied her thoughts now. Her feelings for him had changed, and the boundaries she had built were broken.

The Andheras went out. Pavi went back into the kitchen to prepare dinner. Vivian ushered her inside. The penthouse apartment was posh with teak doors and windows. Intricate carvings added elusiveness to the ambience. Samaira looked around.

"Like it?" Vivian asked her with a hint of anxiety as if her answer mattered to him.

"Yes, of course," she affirmed.

The colourful paintings and the balcony garden made the house into a "home." She stood mesmerised. "I love it, Vivian. How large is your place?"

"Five rooms, plus one for Pavi Ma," he told her.

"Six? Are you serious?"

"Yes, one for me, one for my parents, two for the guests, and one that Kushi uses when she comes."

"Is Kushi staying here?" Samaira did not know that.

"Yes, where will she go? She is like my cousin, Sami," he argued.

With her insecurity earlier, she would have been threatened by that piece of information but not now. "I understand, Vivian. You don't have to explain yourself to me. Why did you not tell your parents that I was coming?"

He tapped her forehead playfully. "Use your brains, Sami. We have planned a surprise party, and if I told them that I was bringing my friends, they might have figured it out . . . which reminds me I have to change Pavi's dinner arrangements."

She pouted. Did Vivian just friend-zone her again? She did not know.

He called out, "Pavi Ma!"

She came running to them.

"*Arre*, what is the rush, Pavi Ma? Please don't cook today. I have ordered from the restaurant."

"My *rotis* will be really good." She sounded upset.

"It is not about your *rotis*, Pavi Ma; we have planned a surprise party for Ma and Pa."

"Oh, that is lovely. I will help," she volunteered.

"Let me get the details together and then call you. You rest until then."

Pavi Ma grinned. "Thank you, sweetie. Do call me when you need me."

She went out, pinching his cheeks. Samaira laughed. "Sweetie?"

"Only Pavi Ma can get away with calling me sweetie," he threatened.

"I have other nicknames for you," Sami teased.

His mobile phone rang, interrupting his retort. He answered.

"Yes, Vivian here. Is it ready? Problem with delivery? Hmm . . . okay, I'll come and pick it up."

He turned back to Samaira. "Problem with the cake delivery. You wait for me, Sami. I have to go, but I will be back in ten minutes."

He grabbed his car keys and with an apologetic look he suggested, "Sami, you better wait in my room upstairs . . . first room to your left."

"Don't worry. I will entertain myself. You bring the cake," she assured him.

"That is my sweetie," he told her.

Vivian rushed out as she threatened to take a step towards him.

She wondered if she should wait for Vivian in his room as he had suggested. Her mind was in a dilemma, but her curiosity got the better of her. Taking the steps two at a time, she reached his room with a racing heart. Loaded with expectations in her mind, she opened the door. The room was neat and tidy. The ivory walls with grey curtains added elegance to the room. There was a big balcony overlooking the lake nearby. Scenic beauty dominated her vision as she took in the lush grass adjacent to the lake.

"Wow!" she gasped. She explored further. There was a bookshelf, and being a bookworm, it was the most attractive feature in the room for her. She examined his collection. From motivational books to romance, it had everything under the sun. The top row comprised of mystery and suspense. She bent down to look at the second shelf.

Twenty Ways to Tune Your Voice. The title attracted her, and she pushed the other books aside to pull it out.

Plop! An old notebook fell out. She picked it up and dusted it. The cover read, "Vivian ————"

"Oh, Vivian's, but why no surname and only dashes?"

Feeling like an intruder, she decided to close it as her conscience won. But a strong wind gushed through the balcony, and the pages fluttered open. She tried her best to save the pages of the torn notebook when one statement caught her attention.

Kavi Ma, I miss you.

She gasped. What did he mean? Something was wrong.

Oh God! He appeared proud, but his life was not as normal as he projected. She felt the strong urge to know everything about him. Had he missed something in his life? If so, she wanted to make up for that!

That thought overrode her guilty need to give his notebook the privacy it deserved. The wind subsided gradually. She settled herself comfortably in the chair on his balcony with the notebook. Her hands trembled as she flipped open the first page. It began with a note of acknowledgement.

Mrs and Mr Andhera, you are everything to me now, and I am indebted to you forever. Whatever you want, whatever you need—even if you demand my life—I will present to you on a platter. I have no words to express my gratitude for you.

Samaira frowned. She loved her parents, but she had not written notes of gratitude for them as a child. Something did not add up. She turned to the next page dated ten years ago. As the mystery unfolded before her eyes, her eyes were glued to the page and she read the feelings of a teenaged Vivian.

I am penning the events that taunt me even today, as recommended by my therapist to overcome my depression. Thanks to the Andheras for arranging one.

The notebook was the result of his therapy ten years ago. She had also heard that writing about the traumatic events in your life would lessen your sorrows and allow you to move on.

This happened when I was a little more than four.

My stomach growled in hunger. I felt tired, desolate, and lonely. Kavita Ma had still not come back. It was almost ten o'clock at night.

I shivered in the cold, in my torn trousers, and my eyes anxiously searched the streets for signs of Kavita Ma.

She limped to me, holding a small dabba[20] of idlis[21] and rice, mixed. She did not have a leg and a hand. I didn't understand why.

"Here, beta[22], have this. I am sorry, this is the best I could get today," she said.

To me, it was like eating a divine meal. I had not had anything to eat the entire day and I was starving.

"Have you eaten, Kavita Ma?" I asked.

She nodded, but I had my doubts. I was not her responsibility, yet she made sure she fed me each day at least once.

She had found me in a dustbin. Yes, I was found sleeping inside a dustbin on the streets of Mumbai. Kavita Ma had picked me up. She had fed me when she got food. Together we had roamed the streets of Mumbai, begging for food.

My mother . . . or, to be precise, the woman who gave birth to me . . . had thrown me into a dustbin and fled. Her lover had probably deserted her, and she didn't want me. That was what Kavita Ma had told me when I asked her about my real mother. I never missed her, though—not even once; Kavita Ma made sure of that.

Many a time, she had fed me the leftover food and had gone to bed with a glass of water. We slept on the streets along with others like us. When the police chased us, we slept on the next street we could find. If it rained, we slept in the rain.

I still remember the day when Kavita Ma's other leg broke. It was an awful night. I woke up to a sharp cry and the thrashing from the police. They chased us away from the pavement. I turned to Ma and

---

20 A metal box used to transport hot food, either from home or from a restaurant, to a person's place of work.
21 A South Indian steamed cake of rice usually served with *sambhar*.
22 Son.

saw her twisted legs. I felt her pain and retaliated. I bit the policeman's hand.

"You little pest! We are doing our duty. Get out of here!" He hit me on my face. The officer shook me off. I fell and banged my head against the lamp post.

I grabbed Kavita Ma and dragged her away from the police while they were busy dealing with the other people. I was almost five by then. I knew I had to take care of her from then on.

The owner of the teashop on the street where we slept was kind-hearted. He gave me some money for the chores I did for him daily. I learned the business from him. He had me enrolled in the government school nearby, where the education was free. If I had some doubts with my lessons, he helped me out. I did not want to miss out on any opportunities in life. I brought food for Kavita Ma—mostly buns from the teashop.

But I longed for her to walk again. I worked day and night and saved every paisa my owner gave me. I had Rs.500 with me when I took her to the hospital.

They told me she had a disease, which I was not able to pronounce. But I understood that her days were numbered. I cried . . . I kept crying. She hugged me. I had almost given up then. Her words changed my life.

She told me, "Beta, I agree that life has been tough so far. But we were happy."

I eyed her in apprehension.

She continued, "We walked through the grass, we slept under the sun, we drank water from the lake . . . who else would get such an opportunity? Not even the richest."

She changed my perception of the way I looked at life. I wanted to help her, but I was helpless.

"*Appreciate the beauty of life, beta.*"

I took her advice to heart. The next day, I saw her talking to a couple who had parked their car at the other end of the road. That is when I saw the Andheras for the first time. I went to her. She coughed, and it took her a minute to get it under control.

"*Kavita Ma, are you all right?*" *I demanded.*

"*Yes, beta; don't worry about me,*" *she chided.*

"*Too mature for his age,*" *she said, affectionately ruffling my hair. The other couple eyed me curiously.*

"*You have a new family, you lucky one!*" *She hugged me.*

"*I don't want to leave,*" *I protested vehemently.*

"*Why?*" *Her query sounded simple.*

"*I don't want to leave you, Kavita Ma.*"

"*I don't have very long to live,*" *she protested.*

"*I know that, and that is why I don't want to leave you.*"

She held my face and whispered in my ears. "Beta, opportunity knocks only once. Don't let it go by. These people are genuinely nice, and they are impressed with you and your attitude."

"*I don't care,*" *I denied.*

"*Don't you want to make your life better?*"

"*Yes, I want a better life, but for you, Kavita Ma!*"

My exasperation was evident in my face.

"*There are thousands of Kavita Mas around; help them but first, help yourself.*"

She turned to the Andheras and conveyed, "He has agreed to come with you tomorrow evening. He must inform his workplace too. I request you to legalise everything. He is a smart and intelligent boy."

They left happily. But I was not happy with her decision. I had decided that I would not leave. I returned in the evening, only to see the municipal corporation people cleaning up her corpse.

I stood there crying for her. I told them to stop, but of course, they did not. My heart ached for the person I had lost, the person I considered as my mother. I still wonder whether she ended her life for my sake. But I will never know. Till then, I had hated God. But I realised that he had always been around me . . . but in different forms—as Kavita Ma when my birth mother deserted me . . . as the tea-shop owner to lift me up and now, as the Andheras.

The car stopped. It was the Andheras. They got out of the car and took my hand. I walked with them. Perhaps it was better to follow Kavita Ma's words. They were a middle-class family with no children of their own. They legally adopted me. It wasn't easy as I did not have a birth certificate. The day I was found in the dustbin became my birthday. But, Kavi Ma, I missed you so much. I never forgot your words. The Andheras gave me everything. Food, education, and clothes. We moved from Mumbai to Bangalore to a new life. Mrs Andhera – Gauri Ma, was always there for me, making sure that I didn't miss Kavi Ma. She has done so much for me. Not even once has she made me feel that I was not her child by birth. With her, I learned that being a mother means more than just giving birth. Though not poor like Kavi Ma, she was from the middle-class. And as her son, I want her to have a better life. She deserves that.

I promise, Gauri Ma, anything for you . . . anything your heart desires, anything to make you happy, anything—even if it kills me to do it. Love you, Ma. Without you, I believe that I might still be roaming the streets in Mumbai. Venting out my feelings has made me feel better.

Samaira closed the notebook. Her eyes were wet. Tears flowed down her cheeks.

Whenever he advised her, she had always thought that it was much easier to talk when things are good for you. But sticking to your values when you are down in the dumps was hard.

And he was a small boy. How much he had suffered to get past all his troubles! Her difficulties appeared tiny in front of his. He had tackled everything with a smile and had embraced life . . . just like his Kavita Ma. She felt guilty about the way she had handled her life. But Vivian had it rough. She could not imagine the anguish he had gone through. He had slept on the roads. But now . . . she looked around his room. The velvet bed and the décor reminded her of a king's bedroom. He had made diamonds out of the stones that life had thrown at him. She felt goosebumps all over.

Her heart went out to Kavita Ma, and she was proud of Vivian. She applauded herself for her choice of a man who had a character of gold. She would never let him go, no matter what happened. In return, she would give him everything he had missed out in his life. Love, love, and more love . . . she promised herself. She had got back on her feet because of him. But now it was her turn to give it back to Vivian—in the form of the love he truly deserved.

CHAPTER ELEVEN

THE FINAL WISH

*Love compels us to break the boundaries and go beyond
the skies. With fire in our eyes, we surge towards our
goals for a smile of appreciation from our beloved.*

She put the notebook back on the shelf where she
had found it. Vivian sauntered inside.

"Sorry, I was late. What did you do?" he
asked.

Her face reddened in guilt. "I was admiring
the view of the lake," she said, pointing towards
the balcony.

Vivian's traumatic past taunted her. She
yearned to pamper him with her love and
affection. She wanted to crush him in a hug.
Most importantly, she must talk to him about her
growing feelings for him. She promised herself
that she would do it today after the party.

To calm her chaotic thoughts, she leaned on the balcony and gazed at the flora outside. Vivian came and stood behind her. She was tall, but Vivian's height and muscular build made her look petite and delicate beside him. She felt his breath on her neck. She sensed the warmth that emanated from him and became feverishly alive.

She turned halfway to look into his eyes. His index finger pointed to the lake.

"I would love to stand here with you every day appreciating this beautiful view. Do you know that, Sami?"

The rustling sound of water and the chirping of birds added enchantment to the place.

She wanted the same and agreed with a glint in her eyes. A wave of tenderness passed through them. Vivian removed the scrunchie from her ponytail.

"Let your hair free, Sami," he murmured into her ears. He inhaled the fragrance of her hair which almost reached her hips, and stroked it, smoothing its length. She stayed within his hold, and his arms cocooned her. His fingers traced her cheeks and the sides of her arms. She shuddered in response.

"Are you feeling cold?" he demanded and pulled her inside the room.

"No, Viv, I want to stay here," she told him firmly. *With you. Forever.*

He outlined her eyes and lips as if memorising the shape. She shut her eyes, loving the heady sensation that filled her.

"Look at me, Sami."

He turned her around to face him. With eyes filled

with longing, he gently lifted her face. His lips kissed her chin tentatively. She sighed. Holding her hips, he kept her captive. His mouth touched her temple, and he warned, "I have to kiss you, Samaira . . . or I will go mad."

Her arms were wrapped around him. "I want you to," she replied with passion.

"Are you serious?"

"Never more so in my life," she reassured.

Their lips met forcefully with passion. Desire coursed through her, and she ran her fingers through his hair. Their hearts beat in a wild rhythm. His fingers caressed her jawline, and she was aware of the heady aroma of his shaving gel. With quickened breath, she kissed him back fiercely, pouring all her love into it.

They were in their own world. The highly charged moment rattled her nerves, but it did not frighten her. Her body was moulded against him. He could feel every inch of her softness, and he hugged her with all his strength. He wanted the kiss to go on forever.

The doorbell rang. He cursed under his breath. The sound brought her back to this world. She tried to wriggle out of his hold.

Vivian stopped her. "No, you are not backing out again," he warned.

"I did not," she whispered in a throaty voice.

"I will not let you go," he warned her, but the seriousness was gone.

She swallowed nervously. The bell rang again. "It must be Kushi," he speculated.

She nodded as her tongue refused to cooperate with

her. She felt self-conscious after their romantic interlude. She had been a willing participant throughout.

"Let us go," he said, ignoring her discomfiture. Picking up the cake that Vivian had placed on the table earlier, she studiously stayed two steps behind him.

They went down the stairs. As expected, it was Kushi.

"Hey, teddy bear, how did the training go?" Vivian welcomed her.

"Three hours of utterly boring lectures." She twitched her nose and took off her shoes. She handed over the decorations to Vivian and turned to Samaira.

"Hello, Sami, we have planned everything for today. Thanks for joining us."

"It is my pleasure, Kushi." Secure in Vivian's love, Kushi's words did not rouse the green monster of envy in her. But her heart reminded her—they had not yet spoken those three magic words.

"We don't have time, teddy. They will be back in half an hour; we have to rush," Vivian commanded.

"What did you both do all this time?" Kushi asked in an exaggerated tone, with her hands on her hips. Their eyes clashed at her query. Vivian lifted his eyebrows light-heartedly.

"Gosh, I forgot! Do you remember what we did?" he responded to her query with one of his own. Samaira reddened as she recalled their secret moment in Vivian's room.

"We got the cake, Kushi," she covered up, pouting at Vivian for pushing her into the corner.

Pavi Ma joined them as they began to decorate the hall.

The three-tiered wedding cake was placed at the centre. They decked everything in red and white. They adorned the walls with heart-shaped balloons and stuck satin bows in between. The doorbell rang again.

"Oh my, have they returned?" Samaira asked worriedly.

"No, I have invited a few of my friends." Kushi winked.

She opened the door to let in three people. "Vivian knows them. Sami, meet A, B, C . . ." she introduced them to her.

She blinked. "What kind of names are they?"

"Don't confuse Sami," commented Vivian.

"Arpit, Baijan, and Chitra," she elaborated. Dressed casually in T-shirts and jeans, they joined them and completed the setup quickly. The dinner Vivian had ordered earlier arrived.

"Wow, I am tempted." Kushi groaned as the aroma of biryani wafted across the place.

"My teddy is hungry," declared Vivian affectionately. The music system was set up, and everything was in place. They switched off the lights. Only the candle at the centre of the cake was lit.

The doorbell went again. Vivian opened the door. The Andheras stepped inside. "Surprise!" they bellowed, and Arpit popped the party popper.

"Wow!" exclaimed Mrs Andhera, looking stunned.

"Happy silver anniversary, Ma!" wished Vivian.

"And you too, Pa," he added and bent down to touch their feet.

"Bless you, Vivian; we are so proud of you," said his mother.

"Happy anniversary, Auntie and Uncle," the others wished in unison.

With tears in their eyes, they took in all the arrangements. "It looks lovely. Doesn't it, Gauri?" Vivian's father turned to her.

"Yes, Amitesh. They have taken only an hour for all the arrangements," complimented Mrs Andhera.

"Come, it is almost seven. Let us cut the cake and have dinner."

They switched on the lights. The applause went through the hall like exploding fireworks. Gauri fed a piece of cake to her husband. Love glittered her eyes. Amitesh handed her his gift of love.

"Wow, more surprises!" declared Gauri.

"Open the box, Gauri. Wear it for me."

Amitesh's love was evident even after twenty-five years of marriage. Samaira moved forward a little, intending to assist Gauri to open her present.

But Vivian clasped her hand and signalled *no*.

She turned to him with a questioning look.

"Their moment . . . let them enjoy," he told her. He rubbed his fingers over hers in an intimate manner. She blushed and moved away from him.

"Let me see how far you can run," Vivian taunted her with his eyes.

She averted her gaze. "Come on, Sami, look at me," he willed her to look at him.

She did the same. "We will celebrate our love like them after twenty-five years," his eyes conveyed. All her troubles melted away.

Everything would be all right, soon. A new life . . . a new love . . . a singing career.

Her heart jumped at that thought, and she whistled in happiness.

"Join us for dinner," invited Vivian.

Gauri went to the kitchen to confirm that they had ordered enough food for everyone. Being a host for years had her tuned to being prepared for all the possibilities. Everyone gathered in the dining room. Pavi served them. The dining area was visible from a large window in the kitchen.

Samaira joined Gauri to help her out in the kitchen.

"May I help you, Auntie?" she asked her.

"No, Samaira, go and have your dinner. I know that you are not merely an employee. Vivian doesn't invite his employees home. You must be a good friend. Am I right?"

At Samaira's nod, she added, "I will not disrespect his friends. I came here just to check if everything is fine."

"Auntie, I will not go anywhere. It is your day; you have your dinner first," she stressed.

Noting the determination in her eyes, Gauri laughed. "Okay, fine. Let us do the 'checking' together; it will hardly take two minutes."

They completed their task in a minute. "Everything is fine. Let us go, Auntie." Samaira tugged at Gauri's hands.

But Vivian's mother halted her stride as she saw Kushi and Vivian sitting next to each other.

"Look at them; they are made for each other," Gauri remarked.

Samaira's enthusiasm dwindled as they observed the pair at the dining table.

Kushi held a piece of *roti*.

"Not so fast, teddy; wait for Ma to join us," Vivian warned, holding her hand.

"I tried to but look at my stomach." Kushi pointed to her tummy.

She dragged his hand over her stomach. "Feel it rumble," she insisted.

Vivian was not convinced.

"You overworked me," she argued.

"Poor girl; I will make it up to you." He kissed her hands.

Her lips drooped down.

"Okay, don't pull that act on me, now. You can have the *roti*." He gave in with a sigh.

He fed her a piece of *roti*, and Kushi smiled brightly.

Like a chain reaction, Gauri smiled too.

"Vivian is like putty in her hands," she remarked.

"Vivian . . . putty?" queried Samaira with a disbelieving look. Her heart refused to accept Gauri's words.

"Vivian is your friend, right? So, you will obviously support him," she mocked, affectionately.

"Auntie."

"I appreciate you for standing by your friend. Vivian had a tough life, Samaira."

Samaira nodded as she thought of his past.

"But do you know who needs his support now?"

"*Me*," she wanted to shout.

But she shook her head instead. Every second of the conversation crushed her heart. She felt attacked emotionally.

"Kushi," whispered Gauri.

"She is my best friend's daughter. She lost both her parents in an accident recently."

Samaira's heart went out to Kushi. Though they sailed in the same boat, she applauded Kushi for not losing her cheerfulness, despite her sorrows.

"Except for my family, she doesn't have anyone. I don't want to leave her all alone to face this evil world," she confided.

"But I can't bring her here. Vivian is single, and society talks."

"So, are you planning to get her married?" suggested Samaira.

"Yes."

"That is good news, Auntie." She hugged her.

"I want her to marry Vivian."

Samaira gasped. "But Vivian . . ." she stammered.

"*Arre*, Samaira, by now you know your friend quite well, or he would not have invited you to his party. He is attached to her and loves her. I know that."

Samaira felt as if a hundred kilograms of iron had descended on her heart.

"Do you know what, Samaira? I don't know why I am confiding to you. Probably it is easier to share stuff like this with an outsider," she remarked.

She agreed. That was what she was. An outsider to this beautiful home!

"My days are numbered."

"Auntie." She rushed to hold her hands.

"Shh, Vivian does not know it still. The doctor told me that I have six months of life with me—at the most."

"Auntie, you must tell your son," she argued, forgetting her sorrows.

"He can't play God with my fate. Vivian and Kushi are my protégées. Once I see them married, I will leave this world happily, secure in the knowledge that they have each other."

Samaira's hands shook. Tears welled up in her eyes.

"And that is my only wish," Gauri told her longingly.

Vivian's words in the notebook haunted her. She knew that he would do anything for Gauri Andhera.

I promise, Ma, anything for you . . . anything your heart desires . . . anything to make you happy . . . anything, even if it kills me to do it. Love you, Ma.

"I could tell him directly, but I don't want him to feel pressurised. You are his friend. Could you please convince him to marry Kushi?"

Gauri turned to her with a pleading look. Tears fell from Samaira's eyes.

"I promise you, Auntie, I will do my best," she whispered.

"Ma . . . Samaira . . . come. Let us finish our dinner before it gets cold," Vivian chided and dragged his women out of the kitchen. The food tasted like sawdust to Samaira. She swallowed everything that was put on her plate with difficulty.

How could God be so cruel? How could he snatch everything away from her again? Vivian glanced at Samaira. He knew that something bothered her. She looked as if she had suffered a great loss.

CHAPTER TWELVE

THE BREAKUP

One-sided love is painful. Let the agony transform into effort to attain your dreams and visions.

The party ended with music and dance. They cheered when Mr Andhera took Gauri in his arms. Samaira's heart ached to see distress reflected in their eyes. She was aware that it was their last dance. The rest of the family enjoyed the occasion with no idea of what was going on. Everyone eventually left after dinner. Kushi was off to the guest room, as she was staying the night.

Vivian held Samaira's hands, preventing her from leaving. Unless she made some noise, Samaira knew that she would not be able to make a dignified exit. He was determined to speak with her that night.

"The terrace is the most beautiful part of our home; let me show you, Samaira." He pulled her along with him, ignoring her resistance.

It was nine o'clock in the night. Moonlight illuminated the place. Pretty roses bloomed on one side of the terrace. There was a huge brass swing at the other end. In the centre, was a round glass table with two luxurious sofas on either end.

"I have to leave, Vivian; it is late," she told him.

"Sure. I will not force you to stay . . . not yet." He grinned.

Samaira's heart lurched at his teasing banter.

"Come, let us have coffee before you leave," he urged. Pavi Ma served them two cups of steaming coffee.

"Thanks, Pavi Ma," Samaira said.

"Anything for you, dolly," she replied as she left the place with a smile.

"Hah, you have captured a place in her heart. She has these ridiculous nicknames for people she likes," remarked Vivian.

He took the lighter from the table and lit the candle. The vase had fresh red roses.

"Setting up everything right, so that nothing goes wrong," he clarified.

Oh my God, not today! Samaira's soul whimpered. She could guess what he was up to, and she had to stop him.

"Vivian, I have to leave. I am done with my coffee." She gulped the rest in one go. Hot coffee scalded her tongue, and she yelped.

"Sami, what is wrong?" He brushed the coffee drops

from her lips and passed the water bottle to her. "Drink this water. It will ease the sting of the coffee," he advised, concerned.

Samaira did as she was told.

"If that doesn't work, I have alternate methods to make you forget the pain," he told her.

Pulling Samaira close, he kissed lightly on her lips. She could not take it anymore. His gentleness and love shattered her. She worried that if Vivian continued this way, she might go against Gauri Auntie's last wish by accepting his love. Her heart longed for it, but she just could not give in. Vivian respected his mother, and she would do the same.

Colourful fireworks lit the night sky, gleaming brighter than the stars.

Noiseless, without disturbing others, the glittering colours enthralled her. The fireworks went on for two minutes and together, they watched the sky in wonder. The show ended with red lights forming a big heart. Her heart thudded.

Vivian went down on his knees and opened a small box. "I made this scene perfect for my proposal, Samaira. Each day when I wake up in the morning, I think about you. When I reach the office, my eyes seek your angelic face. When inside my room, I wonder what you are doing outside . . . you haunt me every second. I want to see you smile, see you walk towards your dreams, and I want to be the one to hold you and take you there. I will be there for you if you fall. I promise to be with you always, and all I want in return is your love, Sami. I love you so much that my world is incomplete without you. Do you love me, Sami?"

Taking the diamond ring out of the box, he held her fingers. The breeze ruffled their hair. Vivian had changed his clothes for the celebration. His blue shirt fluttered against his white pants. He put the ring on her finger. Lifting her hand, he kissed it gently. He gazed into her eyes, seeking an answer.

Unable to bear it anymore, Samaira's tears escaped and rolled down her face. She felt as if she had been ripped into two. The perfect proposal from her soulmate and she could not accept. She was tied. Oh, how she desperately longed to shout yes at the top of her voice. She broke down and dropped down to the ground. Her sobs grew loud.

Vivian was perplexed with her behaviour. He was sure that her response would be a big *yes*.

Was something bothering her? "Sami? What is wrong?" he demanded.

She did not respond, and he knelt beside her on the ground. "Tell me, please." He shook her gently, holding her shoulders. She could sense his desperation and was aware that her silence was hurting him.

Wiping her tears furiously, she told him, "I warned you earlier."

Vivian's hand froze at that statement. "What do you mean?"

"Vivian, I told you that I don't believe in love," she whispered.

Seconds ticked by. He did not react. Vivian's silence became unbearable.

She cupped his face and continued, "I never wanted you to get hurt, Viv. But I can never offer you anything other than friendship. I never saw you that way. Love was never in the picture."

She crossed her fingers at the back, hoping that God wouldn't strike her for that horrible lie.

"I don't believe you," he declared firmly, probing into her eyes.

She shook her head in desperation. "This is what I was afraid of. I did not want this to happen."

"Don't give me this crap, Samaira."

"I told you."

"Yes, I agree, but things changed between us. Please don't deny it, Sami," he pleaded.

She looked at him fixedly. He tried to read her thoughts, and she knew that she had to stop him. But how could she when he said nothing but the truth?

"Attraction," she muttered, unable to meet his eyes.

"Don't you dare say that. It was more than that, Samaira; we had everything . . . friendship, affection, attraction . . . the entire package."

"Your imagination is running riot," she denied weakly.

"The only thing we did not do was give our relationship a name. We simply let it remain as friendship." He tugged her towards him. They both fell together, and Vivian swiftly moved on top of her. Balancing his hands on either side, he observed her fixedly.

"Am I just your friend, Sami?"

"Yes," she whispered.

"And you still don't believe in love, right?"

She nodded.

"If that is the case, why don't you stop me, Sami?"

He tilted his head towards her in a calculative move. Her eyes dilated, and she understood his intention. He swooped down to claim her lips.

"Vivian, don't."

Her hands did not push him. Instead, her fingers gripped his face as if she never wanted to let him go. They kissed under the night sky as the stars watched over them. Passion blended with pain. Vivian loved Samaira, but she was stubborn. Samaira loved Vivian, but she could not give in to him. Agony hurt them like hell.

Vivian's voice wobbled as tears filled his eyes. "Don't do this to us, Sami," he uttered.

"Please, Viv, I can't."

He jerked away from her suddenly. Samaira struggled to regain her composure.

"I am sorry, Samaira. If this is your decision, I can't force myself on you," he muttered formally in a bleak voice.

"No, it is all my fault," she denied.

She raised her hands to calm him. But Vivian moved, avoiding her touch. His attitude wounded her. Her watch beeped, indicating that it was ten o'clock. Life had changed dramatically in just one hour.

"They will close the gate of your hostel; let us go," he told her.

"That is okay; I can go on my own," claimed Samaira.

"No one denied that. But I will drop you," he informed her. His tone brooked no argument.

They drove back to the hostel in silence. Their rapport was broken, and Samaira wept tears of blood for their lost relationship. Vivian's face was rigid and expressionless.

She knew that it was a facade and that he was wrecked inside.

I had to do this, Viv, her mind tried to reach his through telepathy.

For you . . . for me . . . for Gauri Ma and Kushi. And I know that you will do the same if you knew Gauri Ma's last wish. I did the best for all of us."

Vivian stopped his car. Her hostel came into view. Her eyes brimmed with tears of pain.

He wiped them away. "Nothing to cry for, Sami. Goodbye. You decided the path of our fate."

"Everything happens for a reason. Goodbye, Vivian."

On that note, she went inside her hostel.

***

When she came out of her relationship with Ashish, she had felt a sense of freedom. She loved the air of independence it gave her. But when breaking up with Vivian, she had a feeling that she had missed something momentous in her life. Her soul hurt, and she cried until there were no more tears left. Thoughts of Vivian haunted her.

He meant the world to her. He had helped her rebuild her life. Her past would have killed her if not for Vivian's intervention. He had changed her perspective on life. Earlier, she had cursed everything under the sun for her bad luck. When she was stuck in that rut, he had told her, "You have to change the way of looking at things around you. Your negativity is destroying you, Sami."

Her mind went over one of their conversations. His words had created a great impact on her mind.

"What is there to change? What has happened has happened, and life will never be the same," she had told him dejectedly.

"Do you know how CT got its big break?" he had asked.

"With the marketing of a chat application."

"Yes, it was a long time ago. When it came to the distribution and usage of the app, I sent out two teams to different areas to investigate. Each team came up with their analyses and reports. Team one reported that since many villages did not have network connectivity, it would be difficult to distribute the application. They suggested we stop marketing the app to cut down the costs."

"What about the other team?" she had asked, curious.

"Team two found an opportunity in the same scenario. With no Internet connectivity in those places, and with limited mobile phones those days, they went to the network providers and bagged their marketing. They connected with the mobile distributors also. Finally, the app was marketed. In fact, we marketed three products instead of one. It was a huge success and formed the foundation for CT. So, it is all about the way you look at things. Don't let pessimism destroy you, Sami," he had advised her.

Vivian's words of wisdom jerked her back to the world of reality. She had to stop floundering in her misery. She examined her life from different angles and tried to take the best out of the situation. She reminisced over each second spent with him, from the day of her interview until she rejected his proposal. At least she had beautiful memories to carry forward in her life.

"Hah," she cried. "That is the best part of this mess."

Together they had redefined love. She would take that with her and move on. She also had the satisfaction that she had not selfishly given in to her desires but had respected Gauri Ma, the woman who had lived for Vivian.

She would use her sorrows to fuel her passion. Her success would bring a smile on Vivian's lips. She wanted that. With that determination, she went to CT the following week.

The marketing campaign for *Awzome* was a massive success. CT signed up five more contracts with multinational corporates. Vivian was away on business most of the time. A new manager was hired for the Ideas division. Samaira worked under him now and moved to the third floor. She went to singing classes in the evening to hone her music skills. She practiced day and night to get over her sadness and forget Vivian. Her contact with him became minimal. No messages, no calls, no chitchat—nothing—except for official e-mails. His proposal and kisses seemed like a distant dream.

A month passed.

Kushi had completed her project, and Samaira hardly saw her in the office. To Samaira's credit, she was making massive headway in her passion for singing. She cleared three more rounds in the top-singer competition at Planet TV.

How she wished Vivian was with her to celebrate her little successes! Did he even watch the show? Most nights, her pillow was wet with tears for Vivian . . . for what might have been. The office atmosphere lost its charm once she stopped reporting to him directly. To her dismay, Shreya quit her job, as she was moving back to her native place. Everything seemed dull except for her friend Preeti, who was excited, as Praveen had proposed to her. Preeti's happy vibes made things tolerable.

Days passed.

She was surprised when Praveen invited her for a cup of coffee over the office communicator. Preeti and Praveen did not have much time for her these days.

Lovebirds. She smiled at that thought.

They met at the relaxation zone. She wore a grey kurta with white leggings.

"Where is Preeti?" she demanded.

"I did not invite her. Things are bad, Samaira," he said, sounding frustrated.

"What is wrong, Praveen?"

"Preeti."

"What happened to her?"

"She does not talk to me."

"Oh." Samaira was surprised. It seemed weird to her because Preeti was obsessed with Praveen.

"She does not reply to my messages . . . nor does she answer my calls," he complained.

"Lovers' tiff?"

"No, but her behaviour kills me," he confessed.

"Her attitude doesn't make sense to me either. She seemed nuts about you," she told him frankly.

"Everything was okay between us until she tried to talk to her parents about us."

Samaira pursed her lips. "Oh."

"And she is not the same after that. She has not spoken to me since," he told her, vexed.

In desperation, he grabbed her hands.

"Please do something, Samaira. She refuses to speak with me, but I believe she will open up to you; you are her best friend," he begged. His eyes glittered with tears.

That was the exact moment her eyes met Vivian's. She drank in the sight of him like a thirsty traveller in a desert. She was seeing him after thirty long days. She yearned for his bear hug more than anything in the world.

She had not noticed him entering the zone. When did he come in? But right now, he sat with a cup of coffee, two benches away from them. Apart from two more employees, the zone was deserted. He sat at the exact place where he had kissed her tears after that disastrous failure on the stage.

His eyes widened at the sight of Praveen holding her hands.

"I did not expect you to move on so quickly," his eyes criticised her.

"No," she wanted to deny, but her mind came up with an idea. If Vivian believed that she had a relationship with Praveen, he would move on and marry Kushi! She enfolded Praveen's hands and gave him the surety he longed for. "I will try my best and find out what is bugging her."

Vivian's hands crumpled the paper cup. Hot coffee scalded his hands, but he was oblivious to it. This was a Samaira he did not know. He chided himself for not understanding her earlier. He should not have crossed the boundary she had set in their relationship. But it seemed like those boundaries did apply to the fellow who now held her hands tightly. In fact, she seemed to be reciprocating. He threw the cup along with the coffee into the dustbin nearby.

Praveen had not noticed Vivian, as he had his back to him.

Samaira's words assured Praveen. Finally, he had found a way to get to Preeti and make her talk.

"Thanks a lot, buddy. This means a lot to me." He stood up and gave her a friendly hug.

She laughed nervously at his response, hoping that Vivian got the message. Praveen walked away. If he had stayed for two more minutes, Vivian had a feeling that he would have slit his throat. He knew that he was being primitive, but he could not help it. His mind reminded him that he had no right to be possessive when she had thrown his proposal in his face.

CHAPTER THIRTEEN

THE BIG MOVE

Decisions or promises made during moments of fury are doomed to flop, forever leaving scars that never heal.

Vivian sauntered over to her unhurriedly. She knew that he would.

"So, Samaira, you conduct your personal affairs at the office?" His sarcasm was evident.

"Not really." She replied vaguely and got up to leave. He caught her hands, preventing her from going. "Am I right in assuming that Praveen is your new scapegoat?"

Her heart broke. Vivian had never spoken to her like this—mockingly.

"Assume whatever. Hello to you, too," she wished him back sardonically.

"Don't show your civility, Sami; I know you."

"Had you *really* known me, you would never taunt me this way," she retaliated.

"What am I supposed to think when you are all cuddly with your boyfriend?"

"You think everyone behaves like you."

"What is that supposed to mean?" demanded Vivian. She attempted to thrust his hands away.

"Oh no, you don't." He pushed her back into the seat.

"Please let go of me, Vivian."

"So that you can rush into Praveen's arms?"

"Even if I rush, what is it to you? We are not bound to each other." her words came out in anguish.

"Was Praveen your reason for rejecting my love?" He looked straight into her eyes.

"I . . . yes." She looked at the floor, uncomfortably. Lying was hard for her.

He cupped her cheeks, lifting her face to look at him. "I need the truth, Samaira."

"It is the truth," she said with conviction. He bought it the second time. His hands dropped away.

"Okay. I will not fight for a love that is all one-sided," he conceded and stormed out of the relaxation zone.

***

Samaira and Preeti met at the cafeteria for lunch. Praveen did not accompany them, giving them space to talk.

"Preeti, what happened?" she inquired as they opened their *tiffin* boxes.

"Nothing . . . everything is fine," her friend muttered, unable to meet her eyes.

"Don't give me that, Preeti. Praveen is worried about you."
Her eyes widened at the revelation.

"What did your parents say?" she asked.

"I did not talk to them," whispered Preeti with a sigh.

Samaira waited for her to continue.

"Oh God, I am scared, Sami. I honestly don't know how they will react. I don't have the guts to tell them," she conceded in a small voice.

"If that is your problem, you should have told me," complained Samaira.

"I wanted to, but I did not want to trouble you," she replied.

"What are friends for? If you are scared, together we will convince your parents."

"What is the plan?" asked Preeti.

Samaira smiled at her eagerness.

"I will meet your parents along with Praveen. That will help your parents have a look at their future son-in-law." She winked.

"Will that work?" doubted Preeti.

"I hope so," she convinced.

"Thanks a lot, Sami."

"You can thank me after the deed is done."

Preeti laughed. "Yes, and we will party after that."

"Your parents are at home today, right?" Samaira wanted to confirm.

"Yes, they are."

"Meet us at Hotel Bellbirds, adjacent to your house, at 7.30 p.m. After the discussion with your parents, we will wait for you there," concluded Samaira.

***

Samaira looked at her watch. It was 7.30 p.m. She had an eye on the restaurant's entrance. Praveen became impatient. He was dying to break the news to Preeti, but there was no sign of her, yet. Their half-finished coffee was almost cold.

"Did you call her?" demanded Samaira.

"Yes, she told me that she would be here soon."

She glanced at the entrance again. She could not believe her eyes as Vivian and Kushi strolled in. They were dressed to kill and made an exceptional pair. He wore a grey coat that went well with her frilly black evening gown.

"Wow, they look elegant," commented Praveen. Their arrival had attracted the attention of everyone at the restaurant.

Vivian noticed Samaira and Praveen together with their coffee cups and frowned.

Samaira's self-control slipped. She turned away. She would not allow his involvement with Kushi to spoil her happiness.

Kushi looked at Vivian. She followed his gaze to see that his attention was riveted on Samaira and Praveen. Vivian had been completely unhappy the past month. His workload had doubled, and she felt bad for him. Something bugged him, but he never talked about his personal issues with her. She had forced Vivian to accompany her to Bellbirds for a change of scene.

Watching Samaira and Praveen, she could understand the reason behind the change in Vivian. She had gone through the same when Amar chose his career over her and went to the United States. Vivian had been her tower of strength at that time. Without his friendly shoulders, she would have never survived. And she could relate to the pain of getting ditched by the one you love. She looked at Samaira, who was in a deep discussion with Praveen. If nothing else, she would at least keep Vivian's pride intact. He deserved that. Before he could break down, she put her arms around his waist and pulled him closer. That moment caught Samaira's attention. She gasped. Kushi's possessive arms confirmed their relationship. It ripped her heart. She wanted to plead a headache to her friends and leave. Preeti joined them, unaware of the sadness that taunted Samaira.

"Wow . . . are we about to hear wedding bells from our boss's chamber?" She winked.

Samaira's love for Vivian was a secret. Her friends did not know, and the irony was that even Vivian did not know. She would make sure it stayed that way. At least, Gauri Auntie would breathe her last in peace.

Praveen confirmed to Preeti, "Not sure about the boss but definitely from our end."

"I can't believe this," whispered Preeti.

"But it is true, Preeti. Your parents are impressed with Praveen. The wedding date is fixed. They did not want to wait," added Samaira.

"Wow, Samaira, you did it! And, Praveen, you are hooked now. I never believed that you would both come back with the wedding date!" she screamed in happiness.

The last line reached everyone in the hotel, and a few cheered. Vivian put his glass down in exasperation. Praveen and Samaira were getting married! He could not believe his ears.

He thought he would wait for Samaira until she came back to her senses. He believed that she loved him despite her words. His heart crumbled.

Kushi gasped.

"One more shot," ordered Vivian.

"Enough, Vivian," said Kushi and pushed away the small crystal glass.

He had done so much for her. He was there for her when her love had failed miserably. And she did not want Vivian to go through the same heart-wrenching agony.

"I need it, Kushi; be a sport." Vivian dragged it back towards him.

"This is the last one," she warned him.

"Cheers," he said. Before he could order the next one, Kushi pulled him out of the chair and tugged him out.

"The lovebirds are leaving," observed Praveen.

He was happy, and he wanted the entire world to be happy.

"They could not wait," said Preeti, embarrassed.

Samaira stood up, unable to hold her composure anymore.

"What happened, Samaira?"

"I will leave you guys to enjoy your moment," she announced.

Kissing Preeti's cheek, she waved them good-bye and left.

***

Kushi and Vivian parked the car in the apartment's basement.

As she was about to get off, Vivian asked her abruptly, "Are you over Amar?"

"I am trying to be," she replied truthfully.

"I am doing the same with Samaira," he conceded.

Kushi knew that.

"Gauri Ma asked me to marry you," he informed her.

"Oh . . . what did you tell her?" Kushi frowned.

"I did not give her an answer. So, she gave me time to think about it. She told me that if I agreed, she would talk to you," he informed.

"I had no idea that Auntie had this in mind."

"The way she spoke, she had only this in mind. She told me that her dream would be fulfilled if we tied the knot."

"Hmm, tough. We never saw each other that way, right, Vivian?"

"Yes . . . but before I could speak to her, she shivered and fainted."

"Oh my gosh! Yes, her skin is pale, and she is not as she was before; she looks tired," remarked Kushi.

"I was with Ma . . . Dad had a discussion with the doctor and told me that it is because of low pressure."

"Oh, poor Auntie." Kushi's concern was genuine.

"After he came out of the doctor's room, Pa asked me the same—about marrying you."

"What did you say?"

"I told him that I would think about it."

Kushi sighed.

"You are trying to make a life for yourself after Amar.

I want to do the same. This heartbreak is eating me alive." His voice was dry.

"What do you suggest, Vivian?"

"Let us go with Ma and Pa's decision. Are you okay with it? But I must warn you—I cannot promise you grand love. Think about it. At least it will make *them* happy," he suggested.

Taking the elevator, they reached the apartment.

Gauri opened the door. "How was dinner?" she asked.

"As usual," commented Vivian.

"But you are drunk, and that is unusual for you," criticised Gauri.

"*Ma.*"

"We were celebrating, Auntie," Kushi told her.

"Celebrating?" Gauri squealed.

"Yes, Auntie, I have accepted Vivian's proposal."

Vivian's eyes met Kushi's, puzzled. She nodded her head in agreement.

"Yes, Ma, and I want you to eat well and stay healthy for the wedding," he commanded.

Mr Andhera came to them. "What is all the excitement about?"

"Kushi and Vivian are getting married, dear." Gauri's eyes welled with tears of happiness.

"That is awesome," he responded joyously and hugged his wife. "We were hoping for this for a long time," he supplemented.

"You have made us happy. Now I can leave without any worries." Gauri put her hands on Kushi's. Mr Andhera signalled Gauri to stop lest Vivian had second thoughts.

"What do you mean?" demanded Vivian, sharp enough to catch that.

"Nothing; just an old woman's ramblings. But you have made me happy." She put her arm around Vivian and Kushi.

"Pavi Ma!" she called out.

"Sorry for the trouble, but could you please make some milk *kheer*[23] now? Vivian and Kushi are getting married," Gauri requested her.

Pavi gave them a weird look. She knew that Vivian's heart was with the girl who came to the party. But she went off to make the *kheer* without questions.

"What? Are you not happy?" Mr Andhera demanded Pavi.

"No, sir, I am happy . . . happy for Vivian and Kushi . . . but are they happy?" she asked.

"What a strange question, Pavi. Obviously, they are. Vivian has proposed to Kushi," Gauri said, with pride.

"Ma. I am tired. Let me go to my room. Good night."

Vivian took the stairs, two at a time.

"What about the *kheer*?" Gauri protested.

"Ma, I am not hungry," he snapped.

She did not mind his behaviour. With her wish fulfilled, Gauri was happy to celebrate the news with her husband and Kushi.

Vivian locked the door behind him and flopped down on his bed, which sagged under his weight. He needed peace and did not want any interference. The picturesque beauty

---

23   An Indian dessert consisting of rice (or a similar ingredient) and sugar boiled in milk or coconut milk, and often flavored with cardamom.

of the lake did nothing to soothe his volatile mood. The breeze could not calm the fire in his soul.

Oh my, what have I let myself into?

Seeing Samaira with Praveen had triggered his anger, and he had reacted. He knew that Kushi could think only of Amar despite her acceptance of this fake relationship.

Why did you do this, Sami? Was I not good enough for you?

He thumped his fists in exasperation on the pillow. Kushi was like a kid sister to him. He could not even think of her that way. But Gauri Ma had reacted ecstatically to the news. Her pale face had glowed.

Sami, I miss you so much. I can't imagine a life without you.

The mighty Vivian broke down, tears flowing down his cheeks. Covering his face with his hands, his sobs grew louder, and he felt as if someone had slashed him into two halves. He groaned in despair, venting his frustration.

Where did I go wrong, Samaira?

Kushi, who was outside the door and about to knock, paused at the sounds she heard from Vivian's room. Let Gauri Auntie enjoy her "*kheer*" party. He needed his privacy, and so did she. It would take her a long time to forget Amar even though he was the one who had left her.

Gauri waited for the newly engaged couple to get their *kheer*. They did not come down. While twiddling her thumbs, she rang up Samaira. She had got her number at the party that day.

CHAPTER FOURTEEN

THE AGONY OF BROKEN LOVE

*I thought we were different and what we had would last
for eternity, but when it ended the same way as the others,
I realised that maybe they had thought they
were different too.*

Kushi stared at the ceiling, longing for Amar's love with tears running down her cheeks. She had left Gauri Ma waiting with her *kheer*. Probably, she should check if she was still waiting for them.

"Hello." Samaira picked up at the third ring.

"Samaira, this is Gauri Andhera . . . Vivian's mom."

"Tell me, Auntie. How are you?" she asked her gently.

"What could go wrong when I have lovely people around me?"

"You are lucky to have Vivian with you, Auntie," she conceded.

"Yes, and he has made me the happiest person on earth today."

Samaira's heart cried. There could be only one news that could have made Gauri Auntie feel elated. "Has Vivian agreed to marry Kushi?" Samaira's voice stuttered.

"Yes, Samaira, he proposed to her today."

Her hands quivered, and her body trembled. Her foolish heart had fervently hoped that somehow Vivian would find a way to tackle his mother's request and keep her happy but at the same time not give in to her stupid wish.

"Samaira."

She did not respond.

"Are you there?" inquired Gauri.

"Yes, I am here, Auntie," she answered, holding her mobile phone with numb fingers.

"I want to thank you with all my heart, Samaira. I don't know how you convinced Vivian, but you did it; you have fulfilled the wish of a dying woman," Gauri expressed her gratitude with tears in her eyes.

"Auntie, I have to go."

She disconnected the call abruptly. Had she spoken any longer, she would have broken down and made a fool of herself.

How quickly Vivian had moved on after declaring her as the love of his life.

Love had now cheated her twice.

No, don't criticise love. Love did not cheat you; people cheated you in the name of love, her heart chided.

"Vivian, could you not find another way to satisfy

your ma?" she wailed aloud. Her room was empty, as her roommate had the night shift at work today.

I love you, Viv. Please do something.

With that thought, she hit her pillow with her fist in desperation just like Vivian.

I know that I made you leave me, but somewhere I thought you would find a way to come back. I thought you would guide me, love me, and hug me again. I still need you, Viv. I need you more than ever. I need you more than Kushi. I believed that you are the Shiv to my Parvati. I thought we would live like them with the bond of eternal love.

Her vision blurred, and tears took over her. She lost herself completely. Mindlessly, she switched off the lights and did not know when sleep claimed her.

Kushi was horrified. Auntie had blackmailed Samaira into giving up her love. In her defence, she had not known that Vivian was deeply in love with Samaira.

Dying woman?

What was wrong with her? How could she die just like that?

Oh, Gauri Auntie! her heart cried. She was sixty-five. Not the age to die.

But Auntie's actions made sense to her. She had thought of her plight. She assumed that she was doing her best for Vivian and herself after she died. Her eyes clouded with tears. She needed time to think. Her good intentions had destroyed the love between Samaira and Vivian.

***

The next day started out on a gloomy note. Vivian stared at the grey skies that matched his mood. He scowled. Today was Samaira's quarter-finals in the top-singer competition. It was seven in the morning. He switched on the gigantic HD television in his room and played the songs he had recorded earlier on his pen drive. He listened to the songs that she had sung in the preliminary rounds. That had become his daily routine, and he had no intentions of changing that just because he was marrying Kushi. The songs haunted him, and so did her face. Along with the music, her voice made him feel the song. He knew that she was getting a lot of attention with her singing and was a mini-celebrity now. There was an online group dedicated to her. Her videos had lots of views. She had come a long way since the day she had fainted on CT's stage.

And he was proud of her! His Samaira . . .

"Oh, Sami, I miss you."

He hit his forehead to stop his brain from thinking of her. The course of his life had changed, and he had to go through with it. The tune tickled his ears. He opened the notes app and noted down suggestions for her to enhance her tone and the little mistakes she had made in her previous song. Though he was not an expert, he had a knack for judging good music.

He had to pass on those observations to her before she went to the quarter-finals today. He also knew that she had asked only for a half-day's leave in the afternoon as the venue was planned in Bangalore.

He called Samaira. His heart thumped in anticipation to hear her voice. It had been a long time since they had talked.

She picked up with a ghostly hello. "Anything wrong, Samaira?" His senses became alert with her tone.

"What do you want, Vivian? Whatever it is, you should be calling Kushi from now on."

"Kushi is not participating in the quarter-finals today," he countered.

"Nor am I," she responded.

"What?" gasped Vivian.

"I have decided to withdraw from the competition," said Samaira, dully.

"Have you gone mad?" asked Vivian. She did not react. "Are you there, Sami?"

"Yes, Vivian, I have made my decision, and I am sticking with it."

She disconnected the call.

"What kind of a stupid decision is this?"

But Vivian was talking to a dead phone. He got ready to go to work in five minutes. If she had no intention of going to the TV station, then she would be at the office. He had to talk to her.

Buttoning up his shirt, he went down for breakfast.

Pavi Ma brought him hot *rotis* with *aloo subzi*. Taking a bite, he recalled how Samaira had fed him her *rotis* tenderly. His hunger vanished. Whatever had happened between them, he would not let her throw her dreams away.

"Vivian, *Guruji* will come today to find a good *mahurat* for your wedding and engagement. Can you come home by four in the evening today?"

He sighed. "Ma, do whatever you want. Please don't disturb me but check with Kushi once." On that note, he left a gasping Gauri behind. His mind was on one thing: to convince Samaira to get back into the competition.

He left a message for Samaira to meet him in his room. She ignored it. He rang her, and she disconnected. He pinged her on the official communication channel and got no response. Finally, with mounting irritation, he requested Raghu to bring her to his room.

His ever-faithful PA did so, and Samaira did not make a scene in front of him.

"What is the matter, Samaira? Why are you behaving weirdly?" Vivian asked in a controlled voice after Raghu left them. His anger was ready to erupt at any moment.

"To be honest, I don't have the energy to deal with you," she accepted her defeat.

"I have not staged an argument here." His words were meant to be harsh. Samaira observed him for the first time since she came to his room. "Why are you not taking part in the quarter-finals today?" he demanded.

"I don't have to explain myself to you," she remarked.

"Oh God, how you tempt me to throttle you," he growled.

"You forget that I am not Kushi; you don't have any hold over me."

Vivian closed his eyes and counted from one to ten. Never had he felt such scorching anger waiting to explode. "You are a fool, Samaira," he altered his tactics. That caught her attention.

"You got back to your old self again," he criticised.

"Don't you—"

"Don't I what? I speak nothing but the truth. You have

become dull. You have let your personal issues disrupt your dreams again."

"No, you don't understand," she denied.

"I understand you quite well, Samaira. Don't do this to yourself," he added, firmly.

"I don't want to be a singer," she shouted vehemently.

His laughter, laced with sarcasm, rang out at her reply.

"Okay, stop that. I have no mood to sing," she conceded.

"I promised you earlier that I will not let you fall, and I will keep my promise as a friend till my last breath," he vowed.

She gasped at his intensity.

"I will drag you to the competition zone even if it means tying your hands and carrying you there like a cave-man," declared Vivian, thumping his chest.

Silence reigned for a second, and then they both burst into laughter.

Enjoying the beauty of his laughter, her tension drained away, and she felt better after a long time.

"Get ready. I will drop you. Don't get me wrong; I will not cross your boundaries. I want to ensure that you don't run away from the event midway."

She punched his arm, forgetting her troubles temporarily.

She was about to leave when Vivian held her hands lightly. "Sami."

"My only wish for you is seeing you sing in the finals of this competition. If you reach that stage, I will stand with the crowd and cheer for you. I promise that I will whistle for you and when they call out your name as the winner of the title, I will jump with joy and dance like a fanatic fan."

She was touched and gave in, her heart aching. In half an hour, Samaira was ready. Vivian postponed his meeting to drop Samaira. He did not mention any of their personal issues, though it burnt inside him to know her wedding date with Praveen. He pulled out his mobile phone and showing her his notes, said, "These are my observations for the songs you sang for your previous rounds. I am not a music *guru*, but I have just noted down what I felt as a listener."

That gesture moved her so much that she wanted to hug him desperately. He had listened to every line of her song. The comments were genuine, valid, and she would make sure that she would not repeat those mistakes again.

Tears threatened to overflow.

"Hey, I wanted the criticism to push you forward, not pull you down."

"I understand, Viv. My tears were . . . never mind." She did not realise that she had called him Viv. But he had caught that endearment. His lips spread into a smile after a long time.

He parked his car. "Good luck, Sami. Push your personal issues aside. You can deal with them later. Don't bundle everything together and make a mess out of it. Think of music only for, say, three hours? Your shooting schedule is for three hours, right?"

She accepted his sincere advice. What would she do without him?

"Shall I come in to see you sing, Samaira?" requested Vivian.

"Oh, the channel people will not let you in. You should have asked me earlier. I would have booked a slot for you," she told him.

He did not tell her that the CEO of Planet TV was his long-time friend and that he could walk in any time. He had asked her because he did not want to disturb her composure by barging in suddenly.

"That is okay. I will book a slot for the finals. For now, I will satisfy myself watching you on TV. Run inside," he prompted, gently.

She stuck her tongue out and walked away. Vivian parked his car outside. He would wait for Samaira until she came out. A message popped up on his mobile phone.

"Call me, Vivian. It is urgent. Kushi."

He dialled Kushi's number. She picked up immediately.

"Vivian, I overheard a conversation, and I thought you should know about it." She did not even wait for his formal "hello."

"Hello, Kushi, eavesdropping is a bad habit, don't you know?" He laughed.

Being in the company of Samaira for the past hour had lightened him up, and he was in a relaxed mood.

"I did not plan it that way," she protested.

"All eavesdroppers say the same," he sighed.

"Vivian, what has gotten into you? Be serious."

"Okay, go ahead," he invited.

"Do you remember when Gauri Auntie waited for us downstairs with her *kheer*?"

"I know, and I told her clearly that I would not join her. Did you ask me to call you to put me down for that?"

"*Arre*, Vivian, calm down. If you stop me in between, you will lose the love of your life," she cautioned.

"Are you talking about Samaira?"

"Yes." She paused. He was silent.

Kushi continued. "Even though I was not in a mood to celebrate yesterday, I felt bad for Gauri Auntie and went down. I heard Auntie talking with Samaira."

There was pin-drop silence from Vivian's end.

"Are you there, Vivian?"

"Yes, I am."

"Hmm, Gauri Auntie thanked Samaira for helping her in getting you to marry me."

"What?" Vivian cursed underneath his breath.

"There is bigger news than that. Strengthen your heart, Vivian."

"Tell me, Kushi; I am not a child," he retorted.

"Samaira agreed to her because it was Gauri Auntie's dying wish."

"Did you hear that right, Kushi?" he wanted to confirm.

"Yes, her days are numbered, Vivian, and she thought she was doing the best for us."

"Her days are numbered?" Vivian parroted as if in a trance.

"Yes, I checked with Uncle today. He did not tell me anything in the beginning. Then he realised that I would not leave him until he spilled the truth. He confided in me and the truth is, she has blood cancer."

"What?" He was unable to believe his ears. The world crumbled around him.

"Why did they not tell me?" His voice came out muffled. Gauri Ma's pale face and her frequent hospital visits made sense.

"They did not want to see you unhappy, and they knew that if they told me, I would tell you for sure. So, I was kept in the dark too," she replied, her voice trembling and breaking down. "She has got a deadline, Vivian . . . two more months."

The call got disconnected. Vivian threw down his mobile phone. The cruelty of fate was hard to take. Was it his bad luck? He had lost his birth mother and then Kavi Ma, and now Gauri Ma.

Was he doomed to a life without a mother? He sat there, losing track of time, trying to take in the shocking news. His eyes were wet. His body jerked as reality kicked him hard.

Regaining his senses, he drove back home. Each moment with Gauri Ma was precious to him. His mobile phone beeped. It was a message from Kushi.

"Forgot to tell you. Amar has come back to India. He wants to meet me. Don't know how it will go."

Nothing mattered to him now. He had to meet Gauri Ma immediately.

CHAPTER FIFTEEN

THE SON'S PLIGHT

*When death embraces me, I want to welcome it with a
smile. Please don't cry for me; it is not my end
but a journey towards a new me.*

The moment Gauri opened the door, Vivian
ran to her like a child and hugged her tight. He
sobbed miserably and only let her go when Gauri
coughed a little.

She was surprised. Her strong son appeared
to be completely broken. She ruffled his hair to
soothe him. But his tears did not stop. He cuddled
her again. "Please don't leave me, Ma," he begged.

Worry took over his mother's heart. "What
happened, Vivian?"

She coughed again harder.

"Ma, are you all right?" he panicked.

"You tell me. Is something wrong?" she
asked him, concerned.

"Ma, how could you? You never told me."

She was silent as she now understood what he was talking about.

"How did you . . ." she faltered.

"That is not the point, Ma. You should have told me. I would have arranged the best medical experts for you. Why did you leave it too late?" he demanded in exasperation.

"Because when I visited the doctor, it was the final stage."

"But, Ma—"

"No buts, Vivian. I know the realities of life. Money can't save me, and I accept that."

"I don't," he interrupted.

"Vivian, calm down. Before I close my eyes for the final time, I want to see only one thing: the happy faces of my kids. That is why I wanted you to marry soon."

"I know."

"I have the wedding date fixed, Vivian. *Guruji* was okay with the *mahurat* this Sunday. I don't have much time, and I want to finish this off."

Vivian sighed. How could he explain to her? Was it the right move to tell her now?

His dad joined them.

"Pa, why did you tackle everything alone? You know I am here for you always; why did you not tell me?" he cried.

Mr Andhera hugged Vivian.

"Without you both, I would probably be begging on the streets of Mumbai," he said.

Gauri put her hand over his mouth. "Don't underestimate yourself. You have talent. You have given us more than what we gave you. You are the best part of our life . . . our strong, trustworthy, and reliable son. I know that you would never go against my word."

He nodded with a heavy heart.

What to tell her? How could he stop this wedding?

The bell rang. She wiped her tears.

"I think it is Mr Dasgupta. I requested him to bring *sherwanis* for the bridegroom and *lehengas*[24] for the bride. Since you are here, could you please choose for you both?" she requested.

"Ma, please don't involve me in this. You select the best for us."

She opened the door and let the man in, with his two assistants. They carried big bundles of clothes.

"Thank you, Mr Dasgupta; we were waiting for you," she welcomed him.

"And I have brought the best dresses for the bride and groom," he marketed his entry.

"You open your bundles. We will join you soon," she told him. The three men proceeded to show the delicately embroidered handmade outfits.

"I will be happy with whatever you choose for me," Vivian delegated the duty to Gauri.

"With whatever I choose?" she pressed.

"Yes," he confirmed and went up to his room.

"Even though I chose Kushi and you love Samaira?" she probed.

---

24 A full ankle-length skirt worn by Indian women, usually on formal or ceremonial occasions.

"Ma." He stopped in his tracks.

"Do you love Samaira?"

"Yes, I love her."

"Why did you not tell me?"

"I thought Samaira did not love me," his voice faltered.

"My last wish is to see you and Kushi happy. So, I thought marriage between you two was the only way to achieve that."

Vivian was perplexed. He wondered how Gauri Ma knew that he loved Samaira.

"I had no idea what was in your heart or Kushi's for that matter, but you people sounded affectionate, and I misread the situation entirely."

"Ma, Kushi is like a kid sister to me; I never saw her any other way."

"And *now* my boy tells me," she complained to her husband.

Turning to Vivian, she continued, "When Kushi told me that you had proposed, there was no sign of happiness on either of your faces. Did you know that I disposed the *kheer* in the dustbin on that day?"

"I am sorry," he whispered.

"Nothing to apologise for, *beta*." Mr Andhera put his arm around his shoulders. "That is when your mom came to me, and we wondered why you were not happy with the wedding."

"And I recalled Samaira's weird reaction whenever I talked about you and Kushi as a couple," continued Gauri. Vivian drew in a sharp breath.

"I had asked her to talk to you . . . make you agree to

marry Kushi. I knew you two were close, and I thought you would listen to her. You barely react when I talk about your marriage. But I never knew that you had romantic feelings for Samaira. I thought she was just your friend and that you had eyes only for Kushi. How wrong I was!"

Mr Andhera squeezed her hand. "That is okay, Gauri. Relax . . . calm down."

"When I called Samaira to thank her, I had the feeling that she disconnected abruptly. I noticed the way you guys did not join my celebration. That is when I knew that I had missed something in my equation. Even Kushi is not into this, right?"

Vivian nodded. "Yes, Ma. She loves Amar, but there are issues. You must talk to her about that. Ma . . . are you sad that I did not—" He stopped at the look in her eyes.

"Honestly, I've never been so happy, Vivian. Even if I had a kid of my own, I am not sure he would have been ready to sacrifice his love. You were ready to do it, and Samaira respected my wishes too. She is a good match for you. God will bless you both. Let me discuss with Kushi about her life," she told him.

"Ma." He was touched. "Pa, please give me all her medical reports. I will get the best medical help possible." His tone was determined.

Mr Andhera nodded. Vivian revived his hope.

"Poor Dasgupta; he has been waiting for us for quite some time, wondering whether to break our intense conversation." Gauri laughed.

"So, will you select the dress for your big day now? What about Samaira's?" she inquired with her hands on her hips.

"I will choose mine . . . a lot of things have changed. I have to talk to Samaira," informed Vivian.

"It is all my fault," Gauri said, criticising herself.

Vivian put a finger on her lips. "One more word and I will not eat your *kheer* today," he threatened.

She laughed. "Agreed, but you have to promise me that you will finish all of it."

***

Vivian went back to the TV station. He rang Samaira but she did not pick up. So, he assumed that she was not back still. He waited for her outside. He had to fix two important issues today. First was Gauri Ma's health. He had her medical reports with him. Parking the car at the corner of the street, he rang up his friend, who was a general physician. He briefed him about his mother's sickness and sent him scanned copies of her medical reports. His friend promised to come back with his analysis and his recommendation for a specialist. He would do his best for Gauri Ma but right now, he could do nothing but wait for the feedback.

The second was Samaira. Her actions made sense now. He could understand why she had ditched his proposal. How hurt she must have been! She had done everything for him . . . for his mother . . . and he loved her more for that. His intuition had never gone wrong so far. She did not love Praveen; he was pretty sure of it. Somehow, he had to stop her wedding with Praveen. He had to make her admit that she loved him and only him. He had to do this without admitting to her that he knew what Gauri Ma had asked her to do.

Sami, be prepared. Today you will finally declare what is in your heart. Everything will change. Together, we will do our best to change the fate of Gauri Ma.

When she came out, she was astonished to see him.

"Did you wait for me?" she demanded as she got into the front seat of his car.

"I don't know anyone here . . . maybe you could help me get the number of the beautiful host of this program," he suggested.

"Kushi will be upset," she told him stonily.

"Kushi or you?" he asked her and Samaira was taken aback. It took her a moment to regain her composure.

"No, why would I? If my friend is happy, I am happy. I don't care if you are with Kushi or with someone else. It is all the same to me."

"Hmm . . . so when is the wedding?" Vivian changed track.

"Whose?" Samaira blinked at his query. What wedding was he talking about?

"Don't act innocent. I asked about the wedding with Praveen."

"Oh that . . . the engagement is next week, and the marriage a week after that."

"Don't play with me, Samaira. I will do everything I can to stop this wedding." His tone was stern, as if she tested his patience.

"What has that got to do with you?"

"Are you kidding me?" he mocked.

Samaira gave him a weird look. He bent forward and held her shoulders tightly. "Cancel the wedding," he warned.

"Why should I? Even if I want to, I cannot. What have you got against Praveen marrying Preeti?"

She rubbed her shoulders, easing out the pain of his tight grip.

"What? Is Praveen marrying Preeti?" he asked, confused.

"Yes, what is wrong with that?" she exploded.

"Nothing."

Praveen was marrying Preeti . . . not Samaira. His heart jumped at that.

"So, it is 'Preeti weds Praveen' . . . not 'Samaira weds Praveen'?" he wanted to confirm.

"I told you earlier. Love is overrated. I don't believe in love, and I don't want to tie myself again in the same trap," she answered.

"Hmm . . . Samaira does not believe in love then. Let us see." He traced his fingers across her cheeks and tucked the wayward lock of her hair behind her ears.

She moved away from his touch. "Congratulations, Vivian. Your mother told me the good news."

"Oh, thanks. What else did she say, by the way?"

"What do you mean?"

"Nothing; leave it. Let us get back. Were the results announced for the quarter-finals?"

She pouted and twisted her lips. "Yes, they were."

"Did you clear this round?" Vivian's query was impatient.

"I did, but I was in the elimination zone. You could say that I just passed this round."

"Work harder next time, Sami; I know you can." With those words, he lifted a bunch of wires underneath his seat.

"Ahh!" his scream echoed around the car. Dropping the wires, he fainted, just like that.

"Vivian!" she cried. She looked around for some water. The bottle was empty. His hands were cold. She patted his cheeks.

Was he electrocuted?

She shook him hard. He did not respond. Not even a flicker of his eyelids.

"Vivian, don't you dare leave me!" She panicked. There was no one near them. The car was parked in a secluded corner. She had to get back into the building to get help, but it would take time and she could not leave him alone. She controlled her tears and forced herself to think rationally, but her brain refused to function.

His body appeared dull and lifeless. "Vivian . . . Viv." She shook him hard. His cheeks were red.

She leaned on him. "I can't live without you . . . please come back to me."

She thumped his heart. "Oh God, I am hopeless!" she wailed.

The world around her darkened. She could not imagine her world without him. At that moment, nothing mattered to her. Neither Gauri Ma nor Kushi.

A shoulder bag at the back of the car caught her attention. She stretched to retrieve it. There was an ice-cold water bottle inside. She grabbed it quickly and sprinkled a few drops of it on Vivian's face.

"Come back, you fool." She knew that she was getting more desperate with each passing second. She kept the bottle on the dashboard. Her voice trembled, and her fingers shook with fear. With tears in her eyes, she screeched, "What is wrong with you?"

She inched closer to him and rubbed his hands, hoping to warm them up. But he lay like a stone idol, with his body halfway across the seat. She brushed her lips against his forehead and traced her fingers on his face. A wave of longingness overwhelmed her.

"You cannot desert me. I need you, Viv. I love you . . . I love you so much."

His eyelids fluttered a little. She shook him again.

"You are everything to me, Vivian . . . my friend, my family, and most of all . . . my lover. Do you know how much I wanted to shout yes to you when you proposed to me?" she blabbered hysterically, pouring her soul out to him.

There was a faint movement again. She drew back a little. Grabbing the water bottle again, she poured the chilled water over his head.

"*Wah!*" He jumped up from his seat as though he had really received a shock.

"I knew you were faking it, you scoundrel!" she threw the words at him.

She thumped his chest and kicked his knees. He struggled to hold her still as she edged towards him to bite him.

"How did you fake the chillness?"

"I had the cold water-bottle in my hands earlier."

She hit his arms.

"Stop it, Samaira," he groaned.

"How could someone faint by holding a set of disconnected wires?" he asked her.

"I thought . . . I . . ." Samaira had lost all her logical thinking the moment she saw him faint. She chided herself for being so stupid. She was sure that he would take advantage of her spoken feelings.

"You scumbag, what kind of game are you playing?" she demanded.

"Did you think it was a game?" retorted Vivian.

"What else could it be?"

His hold tightened and she gasped. Kissing her soundly on her mouth, he told her, "I wanted to hear those words from these sweet lips."

"So that you could play with me?" She pushed him away, but Vivian's grip was like a steel band.

"Why should I? You already know that I love you," he whispered.

"You are getting married to Kushi . . . I know that."

"You pushed me to it, Samaira."

"I know." She let out a sigh. "What is the point of talking through this again?" She pushed his chest to come out of his arms.

"The point is that I am not getting married to Kushi. I want to marry you."

"What are you talking about?" she questioned breathlessly.

"I love you, and you love me . . . so why should I marry Kushi?" he asked, logically.

She could not expose Gauri Ma. She shook her head. No, she could not.

"I cannot marry you, Vivian . . . not ever," she whispered.

"'No' is a big word, Samaira."

"I mean it, Vivian . . . I can't."

"Will you not marry me even if Gauri Ma's blessings are with us?"

Her eyes widened in comprehension. "You know—"

"Yes, she told me."

"Oh." It meant he also knew of his ma's sickness.

"And I know about Gauri Ma. But I will try my best; I have pinged all the details to a close friend who is a doctor. He will check and get back to me soon. I am determined to give her the best possible medical help."

Samaira held his hands in support. "I will be with you all the way."

"As my wife?" he questioned her.

"Yes, as your wife . . . and everything you want me to be."

"Oh, my dear Sami, I never thought that my dream would come true some day." He hugged her tightly and did not want to let her go. She was content in his arms until a thought disturbed her.

"Vivian, what about Kushi?"

"Kushi? What about her?" He frowned.

"Don't play dumb. You proposed to her, right? Won't she feel hurt?"

Vivian laughed at her question.

"What is there to laugh?" she probed.

"The proposal was nothing but an arrangement to satisfy Gauri Ma. She loves Amar."

"Amar? Who is that?"

"Amar was her senior in college. They were in love. But when he got a good opportunity in the United States, he chose it, leaving her here. That broke her heart, and I was nursing a broken heart like her with your rejection."

"But you were close to her," she complained.

"*Arre*, Sami, we've known each other since we were kids. She is my mom's friend's daughter. She was the sister I never had."

"Hmm . . . I have to believe you when you say so."

"Don't you know the thumb rule? The husband is always right."

"But you are not my husband . . . yet." She pouted.

"It is just a matter of a simple ceremony; you will be mine soon," he announced, brooking no argument from her.

He took out a small box from the open bag.

Opening it, he pulled out the ring and put it on her finger and kissed her fingers one by one. She closed her eyes as her stomach clenched with a feeling of excitement. She shivered as she felt the coolness of his lips. The diamond sparkled proudly. She felt cherished and contented. She would never forget this moment for as long as she lived.

"You are sweet. I love you with all my heart and soul, Samaira," he reiterated.

"I love you too, Vivian, but don't you dare play games like this with me ever again. For a moment, I thought you . . . you . . ." she faltered, unable to finish what she was saying.

"How will I die without seeing you holding the trophy for the top singer?" he joked, smiling.

CHAPTER SIXTEEN

THE CRASH

*If life is harsh, remember that everything in the Universe
happens for a reason. So, don't give up, ever.*

The next day Vivian went to the hospital to get
the report from his friend. Normally, he rushed
to the office in the morning, but today he had
fallen at Gauri's feet and received her blessings.

He should have done this daily. But now was
not the time to brood over that. He had to do
something. He could not let her die. Get Well
Hospital was one of the finest in Bangalore. His
friend had blocked his calendar specifically for
him.

Having booked an appointment for 9.30 a.m.,
he went in directly.

"Hello, Bala, good morning."

"Hey, Vivian, come in."

"What is the verdict, Bala?"

"I analysed the reports, and . . ." he dragged.

"Go ahead, tell me."

". . . her doctor was right. I am sorry to confirm that she does not have much time left."

"Can nothing be done?" Vivian hit his fist on the table.

"Relax, Vivian," calmed the doctor.

"How can I when my mother is dying in front of my eyes?"

"Medication can't help her at this point . . . nor any treatment. But I was involved in a research study trying to understand the cause of cancer."

Vivian was all ears.

"There was a team that claimed that cancer is just the deficiency of vitamin B17 . . . no definite evidence yet."

"Okay, what should I do?" queried Vivian.

"You could try giving her natural therapies and food rich in Vitamin B17, such as almonds, seeds, sprouts and berries."

"I will do that," he promised.

"But I can't promise any miracles," continued Bala.

"I understand," Vivian replied with unshed tears.

"I have listed a few herbal treatments; you could try that too," he suggested.

He nodded helplessly.

"And I will come home personally to check on her daily," he assured him, looking sympathetically at his friend's pale face. Feeling utterly helpless, Vivian thanked him and left the hospital. Stopping at a nearby supermarket, he bought everything Bala had suggested—nuts, seeds and herbal powders. Taking his bags to the car, he set off homewards.

She had done everything for him all these years . . . bathed him, combed his hair, dressed him, fed him, and given him the best education. He felt helpless about not being able to do anything for her now. With tears in his eyes, he took a deep breath to calm himself. Time was running out. His mobile phone rang. It was his father. He frowned. His father never called him unless there was an emergency.

"Hello, Pa," he answered.

"Where are you?"

"I am on the way home."

"Vivian, Ma passed away," his dad told him directly, without any preliminaries.

"Pa?" Vivian's voice trembled.

"Yes, you heard me. Gauri left us all," he cried.

Vivian's heart splintered into pieces.

"She wanted to see you getting married, Vivian. She did not even wait for that." Mr Andhera broke down.

Vivian's hands clenched the steering wheel. Gauri Ma was no more. She has joined Kavi Ma. Only this morning she had blessed him with a smile. She must have smiled despite the pain.

"Why did you snatch her from me?" he implored the marble statue on the dashboard of his car. He had to get back home quickly . . . not to lovingly feed her what he had bought, but to complete her last rites. The agony speared his heart. His mind was preoccupied with thoughts of his mother, and his attention on the road wavered. He drove like an automaton. He did not notice the mother and her little girl walking towards the car until it was too late.

His senses alerted him at the last moment. As a final

attempt to save them, he swerved his car with all his might in the opposite direction. His car collided with a gigantic tree. The crash rocked the entire road. He was not thrown away because he had his seatbelt on. But his head collided partly against the steering wheel before the airbags could help him. The front part of the car was smashed like a *papad*[25]. People around him screamed. The frightened mother and child heaved a sigh of relief. They understood what a close call they had had with death.

Vivian's heart thudded in relief as pain engulfed him. He felt groggy but his mind reminded him that he had to get back home as soon as possible. Blood oozed all over, and his parched throat longed for water. He felt choked as blackness engulfed him and he lost consciousness. People rushed to the car. One of them dialled the emergency number. The ambulance arrived within five minutes. The traffic policeman picked up the mobile phone that had slipped under the broken seat. He searched through recent contacts. There were two entries: one named *"Pa"* and the other *"Biwi."*

He dialled *"Biwi."* He decided that he needed his *biwi*[26]'s help more than anything to survive. He appeared badly injured.

"Hello." Samaira picked up her phone.

"Your husband has met with an accident."

"Husband?" She was confused.

"His card says he is Vivian Andhera from CT. You are his wife, right?"

---

25   A thin, crisp, disc-shaped food from the Indian subcontinent.
26   Wife.

She did not correct him. "Yes, what happened to him? Where is he?" She panicked.

"He is seriously injured. We have taken him to Get Well Hospital at Whitefield," he informed her.

Samaira ran out of the office. Vivian had told her that he would be back soon after meeting his friend, who was a doctor at the same hospital.

Seeing her running, Raghu questioned her, "What is the matter, Samaira?"

"It is Vivian. He has met with an accident!" she cried.

Raghu joined her. Getting the details of the hospital, they drove the car at breakneck speed to get there.

***

Her heart thumped erratically. The ten-minute drive to the hospital was the longest journey of her life. Just when she thought everything was going to be okay, she felt as though she was back at step one where she had started. Her world shattered along with her dreams and love.

"Oh, Vivian, don't worry. Everything will be all right soon," she whispered to the empty air.

"Whatever God has decided, I will not merely sit and watch; I will fight against all odds," she vowed determinedly to Raghu.

Seeing her tense face, he reassured her, "Don't worry, Samaira. Get Well Hospital is Dr Bala's; he is his close friend. So, Vivian is in the best hands."

Samaira recollected Vivian talking about Bala. He would have visited him in the morning, regarding his mother's medical reports. She turned to Raghu with eyes brimming with tears. "Whatever the case, I will shake him back to his life." Her engagement ring sparkled on her finger.

When they reached the hospital, they rushed inside. They were informed that Vivian was in the ICU and needed surgery.

"That is him." Raghu pointed to a young man, who rushed to the other end of the corridor.

"Dr Bala!" they called, as they caught up with him.

"We are Vivian's friends. Please let us know what happened," Raghu demanded.

He looked at them oddly. Being an industrialist, Vivian was a celebrity in society. His health status should not jeopardise his status or his business.

"Look, doctor, I am his fiancée. You have to tell me." Samaira pointed to her ring.

Noting the resolute look in her eyes, he answered, "See, I don't have much time. Vivian has lost a lot of blood. He has a brain injury, and three clots. It must be operated on as soon as possible. I have called my friend Shiv; he is the best neurosurgeon I have worked with. Nothing to say as of now, except trust us and . . . God."

Samaira stood there speechless. What she had not envisaged even in her wildest dreams was happening in front of her eyes.

"Have you informed his parents?" Bala inquired.

"I will tell them," volunteered Samaira.

"You do that and get a signature from one of them; we need their consent before we start this surgery. Please get it as soon as possible. I will make sure that there is no delay because of that. Vivian is my friend, and I will do my best for him."

Samaira called Gauri Auntie's number. It kept ringing. No one picked up.

"I have Mr Andhera's number; let us try that," suggested Raghu.

"Hello," Mr Andhera answered in a shaky voice.

Raghu did not know how to break the news. Samaira snatched the phone from him.

"Uncle, this is Samaira."

"Samaira, Gauri passed away," he cried, and his sobs echoed in her ears.

"What! When did it happen, Uncle? She seemed fine yesterday," she said, shocked.

"This morning, about an hour ago. Vivian is on his way; he should be here any moment. I am waiting for him."

She had to break the bad news to him. "Uncle, you have to be strong." Her voice was unsteady.

"Vivian's car met with an accident. I am at the hospital with him. He has sustained a brain injury and must undergo surgery now."

"Oh no, not my son too!" he wailed.

"Don't lose hope, Uncle. Nothing will happen to him. You take care of Gauri Auntie's last rites. I will stay with him. Raghu will bring a document to you. Please sign it. It is the legal consent required to perform this surgery," she instructed in a calm manner, careful not to sound panicky.

"Okay, Samaira. Listen, I trust you. Bring him back to me . . . bring him back."

Mr Andhera's pathetic sobs faded away as the line went dead.

"Raghu, go to Vivian's house and get this signed by his father. Gauri Auntie passed away," she informed him, with sadness.

"Does that mean . . ." he struggled to complete his query.

"Yes, Vivian should have known, and I presume that was when he probably had his accident."

***

Raghu came back with the signed document. They began the surgery. Shiv came to the hospital with his team of six doctors. No one was allowed inside the intensive care unit. Samaira observed him through the small circle of glass. His face was pale and lifeless. With the oxygen mask on his face and tubes and cables around him, he looked nothing like the Vivian she knew. She whimpered and hit the wall with frustration. Time ticked on. Each second seemed like an hour. Raghu came back with some coffee.

"Have this, Samaira. Dr Bala told me that this surgery will take some time. Do you want to look at the reports of the scans they took before the surgery?"

Samaira refused both the coffee and the reports. "I am not a medical expert, Raghu. First, let them complete this surgery. I don't want anything until then."

Raghu could understand her love. They were meant for each other. He sincerely wished for his boss's speedy recovery, so that he could reunite with Samaira soon.

After pacing restlessly outside the ICU for an hour, she sat dejectedly on the chair outside. What were these people doing with her beloved Viv? She promised Lord Ganesh that she would offer three coconuts to him if the surgery was a success. She also swore to Lord Shiv that she would fast for him the next *Maha Shivratri*[27].

She got up forcefully and paced, picturing his face and murmured, "Nobody deserves a second chance at life more than you. I know you, Viv; you will come back to me. You are a warrior. Fight for your life. Don't give up; please don't!"

With each passing second, it became more difficult to hold her hopes high, but she was hanging on.

I promised your father that I will bring you back, and I will.

She closed her eyes, and as the clock ticked away, she became more anxious.

Dr Bala and Shiv came out of the OR after three hours. Samaira and Raghu waited nervously, dreading their response.

---

27   A Hindu festival celebrated annually in honor of the god Shiva.

CHAPTER SEVENTEEN

THE HOPE

When life blows out the flame of opportunities, don't despair. You can always rekindle the tiny light of hope that burns deep inside you.

"The surgery was successful. We saved his life. The surgery took about an hour, but we stayed with him for two more to ensure that he is doing okay," Bala told them. "Shiv did a great job, and Vivian fought well. Together, they pulled a miracle." He patted Shiv's shoulder.

Her eyes gleamed, but her premonition warned that something was not quite right. She waited for the "but."

"But . . ." continued Bala.

"We have removed the clots, and he is physically fine. In fact, his eyelids flickered once, which is a good sign."

Samaira prepared herself for the worst.

"But with traumatic accidents like this, we suspect that his brain may not come back to the world of the living," continued Bala.

To Samaira, his words did not make any sense.

"Though he is physically alright, his brain hasn't recovered, and therefore we suspect that he is in a coma."

"What does that mean?" she demanded.

"Calm down, Samaira. Let me elaborate. Vivian is alive, but his brain is functioning at its lowest level of alertness. He may or may not have his eyes open, but he cannot communicate or follow directions." He paused, noting her agonised state, but he had to do his duty as a doctor.

"His brain will not process information in the way it used to," Shiv said.

She shook her head. She wouldn't let this happen.

"Is there a way to come out of this or . . .?" queried Raghu with a heavy heart.

"It depends on his will. Sometimes it just lasts for two to four weeks . . . sometimes years. Instead of recovering, some people move from coma to a vegetative state and pass away," added Shiv.

Before Samaira could explode, Bala continued with the positive aspects.

"But there is always scope for improvement. You must watch for the signs and be positive. If he keeps his eyes open for a longer period or if you can wake him from sleep normally, then there is a definite possibility of him recovering. The progress might be slow, but he may get back his motor reflexes, sense of hearing, and other things back in no time. Hope matters here more than anything else."

"Can I see him?" she asked them.

"You can, but he won't know."

She wiped her tears and went inside. The team of doctors came out, giving her privacy. She stared at Vivian's ghostly face. She felt devastated to see him in this state, and her emotions were in a turmoil. The last time she had seen him was when she had accepted his proposal—and he had a look of joy on his face. His eyelids flickered. She went close to him. He seemed to look beyond her.

"Vivian." Her voice was hoarse. "Are you okay?" she asked, swallowing the lump in her throat.

There was no response. She touched his fingers gently. Tears ran down her cheeks, and she was unable to stop crying. Her heart seemed shredded into pieces, seeing his insipid face and weakness.

"Do you remember me, Vivian?" she asked gently. Her engagement ring glared dubiously at her question. He had given her the opportunity to live her life for the second time, and she would do the same for him.

"It does not matter, Viv. Don't strain yourself," she whispered.

She recollected his promise when she was lost in her life.

You will always have a shoulder to lean on when you fall down with your mistakes.

"It is time for me to promise you now, Viv. You are not alone in this. Fate has presented us with this battle; we will regroup our forces and fight back together. We will be back on track even if it takes a long time. The walk might be tough, but I will be with you through thick and thin. *You will always have a shoulder to lean on.*"

She stared into his eyes, hoping for a miracle.

"You trusted me, Viv. You never gave up on me, and I will never give up on you."

His eyelids closed and she walked out. The doctor kept him under observation for three more days. Except for the movements in his eyelids, Vivian did not show any other signs of improvement.

Samaira requested Dr Bala to send him home.

"Let him be in his own zone," she argued.

"My medical opinion is to keep him here for a month," he retorted.

"Is it possible for you to set up the required medical equipment in his room at home and give him routine check-ups? We could hire a full-time nurse and call you in case of emergencies," she reasoned.

"Yes, but—"

"Doc, he needs to get back to familiar surroundings. Being at home will give him the willpower to fight back, and I will help him do that," she declared with fire in her eyes.

"It might not be easy," he suggested tentatively.

"I know that, but we will come out of this. His ma's blessings will help for sure."

Bala had to acknowledge her remarkable courage and agree. "All right, I will send my team to set up the necessary medical equipment at his home. The rest is up to you. The ball is in your court, Samaira. All the best to both of you."

She nodded with a smile. She turned around to see Raghu checking e-mails on his laptop. He had been there all three days except at night.

"Raghu, you'd better go to the office and take over for

the time being. We should not let work suffer because of this. But let this news stay between us for the moment. I will take him home."

Raghu admired the way Samaira handled the situation. Promising her his complete support, he returned to the office.

***

Vivian was brought home four days after the accident. The last rites for Gauri Ma were all done. There was a picture of her at the centre of the living room, adorned by garlands of roses.

The moment Mr Andhera saw Vivian, he broke down. He cursed God for what had happened. He was filled with anger and he flung the wooden-framed picture of his favourite God, whom he had worshipped regularly, across the room. His son's plight broke his heart.

Picking the picture up from the floor, Samaira dusted it off.

"No, Uncle," she said. She had just got back after collecting all her stuff from her hostel and settling her dues. She was now dressed in a white *salwar* suit for Gauri Auntie's prayers. She did not care about what others would say.

Holding his hands, she reassured him. "Don't cry, Uncle. Blaming God is not the right thing to do. And do you know who told me this? Your son, Vivian."

"I can't bear to see him like this. I have never seen him inactive," he told her.

"Was it tough to move him upstairs to his room?" she asked him.

"Yes, but Dr Bala's team was wonderful. Samaira, I am worried."

"If you worry, will he get better?"

The old man shook his head.

"No negative vibes around him, Uncle. Let us stay positive. Let us do what Vivian would want us to do . . . what Vivian would have done had the situation been reversed."

Her words stirred him.

"And he is a survivor at heart; how could he have fought all those battles on the streets? He was just a little boy, Uncle; yet he had the instincts of a fighter. He will do it, Uncle; believe me. He will not let go of any opportunity that comes his way," she said, reassuringly.

"But the doctor told me that he is unlikely to recover from his coma in spite of his good physical condition."

"True, and I believe it is because he is affected by Gauri Auntie's death. Time heals everything, Uncle. We will find what makes him tick and push him towards it. He will recover for sure," she insisted, more to reassure herself rather than him.

Hope glimmered in his eyes.

"Welcome to my home, *beti*[28]." He kissed her on her forehead. He saw a version of Vivian in her eyes. She was so like him.

***

---

28 Daughter.

She asked Pavi Ma to put a spare cot in Vivian's room. She would not move out until Vivian woke up and asked her to. She pulled up a chair and sat near him. His eyelids were open. She was not sure if it was an illusion, but his eyes appeared bright.

Being in your own zone gives you that lift.

She smiled at her decision of bringing him back home.

"Vivian, I am Samaira," she said. As expected, there was no response.

"How rude of you, Viv! You forgot me so soon." She pouted. "The police called me because you had saved my number as that of your wife."

His gaze was blank, but she continued.

"You are a *sweetie*, Vivian," she told him. With tubes no longer around him, she brushed her lips against his forehead. Bending closer to his ear, she whispered, "But being sweet is not going to help us. We have to stay determined."

"Okay, I will not tax your brain with serious issues today. It's not every day one collides with a tree and ends up in a coma. So, I will let you take it easy today," she said, winking.

For a moment, she thought that his lips curved into a mysterious smile like the Mona Lisa, but it was gone the next second. *Could he hear her? Had she imagined it?*

But she would not speak about her doubts to him. Positivity was the key here, and she would keep encouraging him. And it was probably too early to expect miracles the first day.

"But, Viv." She turned to him again. "No fiancée will get an opportunity to take care of her future hubby like this, and once we are through this, you have to get me . . . hmm . . . let me think. What do I want? How about we celebrate it with *kulfis*? This time you must choose the flavour you like, not order *pista* like the last time," she commanded with her hands on her hips. She continued her monologue.

"Do you remember the last time we had *kulfi* in Chennai? You whispered in my ears that the *kulfi* on my lips tasted better than the one you held in your hand." She pointed her fingers at him playfully.

"Don't think that once you are better you can have your mischievous way with me," she warned him. She reminisced about *that* beach moment and a feeling of longing overcame her. She wanted to hear his rich baritone again.

Kushi entered Vivian's room with a knock.

"See who is here to meet us, Viv; it is our Kushi," she told him.

"Isn't your teddy beautiful?" she continued talking to him, and Kushi understood her intention.

"Viv will never agree that I am beautiful, but Amar would." She pouted.

Samaira lifted her eyebrows. "When did he—"

Before she could complete her query, Kushi said, "He has come back for me, Sami; he has left everything just to be with me."

Samaira hugged her. "We are so happy for you, aren't we, Viv?" She purposely included Vivian in the conversation.

"I was so happy until I heard about Gauri Auntie and Vivian," Kushi muttered.

"Don't spoil your happiness, Kushi. Uncle was all praise about how you have been a pillar of strength for the past three days."

"He always exaggerates. I knew Vivian was in safe hands. This is the least I could do," she protested.

Samaira put an arm around Kushi.

"But Gauri Auntie was like a mother to me," Kushi cried.

"Vivian and Kushi, you both must accept the fact that she is no more. I went through this same agony when I lost my entire family in a day."

She turned back to Vivian. "You told me to move on and not get stuck in the past. Now I want you to do the same. Let us be happy for Gauri Ma. At least she is free from the physical pain that killed her daily."

Holding Vivian's and Kushi's hands with hers, Samaira spoke calmly, "Gauri Auntie wanted both of you to be happy; that was her last wish. She would definitely not want to see her children crying. Am I right, Vivian?"

He closed his eyes as if her speech tired him. She let go of his hand.

"Good luck, Samaira. Vivian needs you now more than ever." Kushi kissed Samaira's cheek.

"It is the other way around, Kushi. I need him. I love him, and I will do anything just to hear him whisper my name again."

CHAPTER EIGHTEEN

THE PHOENIX REBORN

*I am a warrior. I will not die. I might tumble down, but
the fall will never be my end. I will rise like a phoenix
out of the ashes and soar in the sky, taking my
love and life with me.*

The next two weeks followed a routine. Samaira
fed Vivian, as he was now able to eat. He no
longer needed the feeding tubes. He responded
to her touch now, and she was ecstatic. She had
woken him up yesterday by shaking him, and Dr
Bala had assured them that it was a major sign of
improvement.

The next day, she woke up, filled with hope.
The nurse cleaned him and dressed him with
Samaira's help. Together they transferred him to
a wheelchair, with the nurse holding his shoulders
for added support. He was advised not to stay in

bed all day to avoid bedsores, which were difficult to heal. So, they moved him frequently.

Samaira read out the news to him every day. "So, let us see . . ." She rustled the papers to read the headlines. "The government plans to provide smartphones to everyone below the poverty line." She frowned. "I don't think this is a good move. What do you think, Vivian?"

He blinked his eyes.

"Hah, you have become a good boy after the accident. These days you agree with everything I say!" she said, laughing. "But CT could definitely take advantage of this fact . . . our reach for digital marketing will grow farther. You must pay me extra for that additional tip, okay?" She nudged his shoulder.

"Hmm, for some sports news now . . . my cricket team has won the finals. All hail the Chennai team!" She caught the tip of his nose and teased him.

Raghu came in. "Here comes Raghu. Ready for the office updates, Viv?" she asked.

"Good morning, boss." Raghu's voice was cheerful.

"Hey, Raghu, have you brought it?" she asked.

"How could I forget?"

Raghu passed her the display board that Vivian had put up for her at the office.

Thanking him, she turned to Vivian. "I will write quotes for you from today."

"You could probably start with 'Congratulations, CT,'" Raghu suggested.

"Good news?" enthused Samaira.

Raghu nodded enthusiastically and turned towards Vivian. "Boss, you know our marketing campaign for *Awzome* was a massive success and we signed multiple deals after that, but now, impressed by our creativity, we have bagged a big deal with *Star Foodies*."

"That is awesome . . . right, Viv?"

She gasped. Was that a little smile on his face?

"Did you see that? Tell me I did not imagine it, Raghu!" she cried.

"No, you didn't. I saw that too," confirmed Raghu, touched by the incident.

"Mr Patel has confirmed the deal and signed it for you, Viv. Join us soon for the celebration party."

"We will," she assured him.

Preparing to leave, Raghu paused at the door. "Oh, I almost forgot, Sami. The economic federation has nominated Vivian as one of the contestants for India's top ten entrepreneurs; let us wait for the ranking. Topping that list was his ambition when he started CT."

"Wow, congratulations, Viv! You never mentioned that to me," she chided.

Raghu laughed. "One can never satisfy girls, boss."

With a pout, she switched on the television. The past two weeks had been hectic, and she'd had no time for TV. The pen drive was still connected to the TV. Seconds later her voice reverberated throughout the room.

"Oh God!" She sat down with her hands on her head.

Her songs! His love was unparalleled. Her eyes filled with tears. She wrote her feelings on the display board and hung it where he could see it when he opened his eyes.

"Vivian, I love you so much," she whispered the written words in his ears.

She smothered his cheeks and forehead with tiny, feathery kisses. The nurse walked in with a glint in her eyes. "No, you are not supposed to do that," she threatened, shaking her finger.

"Look at her, Vivian; she won't allow your fiancée to kiss you," she complained.

"You can even make love to him, but wait for him to get better," the nurse murmured in her ears. "Now go ahead and tell him what I suggested," she said in a louder tone.

Samaira blushed crimson. She adjusted her *dupatta* consciously. Vivian wriggled his toes.

"Kiss him more; he will get better soon," the nurse said, with a laugh.

"*Arre*, my kisses don't have healing powers, but I believe my songs do." She pointed to the TV.

"Good move, Sami," the nurse appreciated her. They had become good friends.

"Why don't you do a live performance for him?" she asked.

"I will. I forgot to tell you, Viv. The quarter-final rounds are finished for all the regions, and tomorrow I have the semi-finals. I thought of singing a melody, and I need your suggestions."

He did not respond.

"Mark my words. He would make a sweet husband, Nurse. He agrees to whatever I say now. Earlier, he was the dominating type," she remarked with mischievous eyes.

The nurse winked back.

"Hear me out, Viv."

She picked up his mobile phone and opened the notes app. Placing it near him, she said, "You can note down your suggestions as usual. Feel free to criticise me."

She pouted and wriggled her hips. The nurse laughed out loud.

She closed her eyes and began to sing. The nurse was awestruck and captivated by Samaira's voice. The melody went through Vivian's ears, touching his heart.

"Wow, I never knew that you were this good," the nurse commented at the end of the song.

"Sami," the voice was hoarse.

Their eyes turned to Vivian, surprised.

"He called me! Vivian called me Sami!" she wailed to the nurse. She cupped his face gently and gazed into his eyes.

"Yes, he did," the nurse agreed.

"Thanks, Viv; come back to me. You promised yourself to me forever," she whispered to him.

This time, Vivian's smile stayed; it did not go away.

***

The next day, Samaira left for the semi-finals early, after informing Vivian. The nurse finished her duties and left. Preeti called her in the morning to wish her good luck. She could not attend Preeti's wedding with Praveen, which had taken place a week ago. But her friends were understanding and supportive. How could Vivian ever think that she had *those* feelings for Praveen? He was like a brother to her. *Men will be men*, she thought.

Preeti and Praveen made an attractive couple.

Just like me and Vivian. Her heart sighed with yearning.

By evening she had bagged one more success, but her heart longed to celebrate that moment with Vivian. She reminisced about how he had pushed her to continue her singing journey. He was currently making slow progress but the big miracle her heart wished for had not happened. It was almost a month since the accident. Would Vivian stay this way forever? Were their lives doomed to be like this?

But he had called out to her thrice. Bala had confirmed that it was a major milestone in his recovery and had reassured her that he would be all right soon. But that was the issue. Whatever Bala told her was tentative, and she tried her best to make it come true.

Mr Andhera popped in from time to time.

He was gradually coming out of the sorrow of his wife's death. Samaira happily shared Vivian's small movements or his words with him. They kept their hopes alive. Two more weeks passed. Raghu informed them that the ranking for the entrepreneurs was finalised and that the list would be out the following evening.

She pushed Vivian's wheelchair out into the balcony. The cool breeze ruffled their hair.

"Do you remember bringing me here for the first time, Viv?"

Without waiting for his reply, she continued, "We kissed here with the eternal promise of love, Viv. We knew that we were made for each other though we never spoke the words. Let us keep that unspoken promise for the rest of our lives."

Vivian stared at the lake.

"I will love you forever, Viv; you are everything to me," she professed, staring at the lake.

His fingers clutched the wheelchair. His eyes shifted to her. Deep in her thoughts, she did not notice that.

"And our destinies will be decided tomorrow," she mused and turned to him. "You forgot that, right? You have become careless, Viv," she continued her monologue. "The ranking of the entrepreneurs happens tomorrow, and I have got the finals of the top-singer show."

Vivian had a strange look in his eyes.

"Don't give me that look. I am not frightened to face the audience. In fact, I am excited, Viv; it is a big day for me. Planet TV has made grand arrangements for the show. Luckily, it is happening at the Bangalore stadium in the morning, and they are expecting a huge crowd. Along with the judges' decision, the public will also vote to choose the final winner out of the five of us. Will you vote for me, Viv?" she asked him.

She saw the tilt of his head like a nod.

"I know you will; you are my darling." She hugged him. "May good luck be with us." She ruffled his hair affectionately. His hair had grown, and the wind played with it. "I will give you a haircut tomorrow. You must put up with my style until you can get up and walk to the hair salon. So, do that soon if you don't want me to mess up your hair," she threatened him in a playful tone.

Samaira tossed and turned that night. Though she had talked to Vivian confidently, anxiety gnawed at her insides. She desperately wanted to win. She wanted to bring the smile back to Vivian's lips. She wanted to stand tall and make Vivian proud of her. She noticed a slight movement from Vivian's cot. It was dark except for the moonlight that filtered in from the balcony.

Did he just turn over in his sleep?

She was not sure. The day dawned with anticipation for Samaira. She dressed in her lucky *salwar* suit, which her mom had gifted to her last year on her birthday. She knew she had to change again. The channel was taking care of the dress to go with her song along with professional makeup. She was now a mini-celebrity in India. Planet TV had studios in all the big cities. But the ones in Chennai and Bangalore were bigger, and they shot most of their shows at either of these locations. Last year, the venue for the finals had been Chennai, and this time it was Bangalore. She was happy about that. She could get back to Vivian as soon as the show was over.

This was a *free* round, and they could sing any song of their choice in any language. And she had chosen the song that had impressed Vivian at the clothing store and made him declare her as his favourite singer. She bent towards him. His eyes were closed.

"You forgot your promise, Vivian," she accused him.

My only wish for you is seeing you sing in the finals of this competition. If you reach that stage, I will stand amidst the crowd and cheer for you. I promise that I will whistle for you, and when they call out your name as the winner of the title, I will jump with joy and dance like a fanatic fan. His voice reverberated in her heart. She let out a sigh.

"I know that you will not come to whistle and cheer for me, but at least wish me luck," she begged him.

His eyes stayed closed. Seconds ticked by as she stood dejected. She held his hands for a moment.

"I will do my best today, Vivian," she promised. Taking the marker, she wrote, "All the best, Viv; hope you top the list today."

She went to the competition, hoping for the best.

Dressed in a western gown and makeup in place, Samaira waited for her turn. It was a live program, and she was thrilled. Three out of the four contestants had sung beautifully. The audience got to hear four songs from different genres—classical, rap, an old Bollywood song, and one of them had tried a fusion of songs.

She was the fifth and the final contestant. Her stomach flipped, and a thread of fear took over her. She had come a long way after fainting in the company's entertainment hall. She remembered Vivian's words after her failure.

What really matters is what you think about you.

"I am the top singer, and I deserve the title," she repeated the affirmation in her heart.

She missed Vivian . . . his wisdom, his smile, his everything. She wanted to see him once before she sang on that stage. She checked her watch. Did she have time to go home and come back?

"The next contestant on the stage is Ms Samaira Ranjan," the compere Laila announced, with the audience cheering for her. She walked on to the stage.

They had set up a big dais in the centre of the cricket ground, and people cheered for her from the stands. A few people close to the contestants and the TV crew stood near the stage. The electrifying atmosphere chilled her, and she was nervous. Fidgeting with her gown, she accepted the microphone from the organiser. She closed her eyes and willed her tension to ebb away. She badly wanted today to be her day.

But Vivian will miss my performance.

She cleared her throat to sing.

Vivian stood close to the stage along with Dr Bala and Raghu. She blinked hard.

Was she dreaming? Did her heart conjure up the image? She wished desperately for what she saw to be true.

She pinched herself hard. It hurt, and Vivian still stood there. He was fine!

"Oh my God!" She put her hands over her cheeks. The crowd did not comprehend her reaction.

He waved back at her and signalled a thumbs-up. He mouthed, "All the best, Sami."

That was all the motivation she needed. His wishes inspired her to give her best performance. The compere gently nudged her to sing.

Every night in my dreams . . .

The lyrics from the *Titanic* flowed from her lips, and the audience sat spellbound. Every word of the song reminded her of Vivian and their love. For the first time in her singing career, she enjoyed her song more than her enthralled audience. She received a standing ovation at the end. She looked at the blue sky above the stage. She had a feeling that her parents were watching over her. Contentment rushed through her and she felt a deep satisfaction as she sensed their blessings.

"Thank you, Ma, Pa," she expressed her heartfelt gratitude.

The crowd expressed their love for her with a thunderous applause. She pointed the microphone towards Vivian and said, "This one is for you, Vivian."

She saw him whistling from the crowd, cheering for her.

"I fulfilled my promise," his eyes communicated his excitement.

CHAPTER NINETEEN

THE BEGINNING

The end outlines the beginning of a fresh journey towards a life of success and togetherness.

Laila retrieved the microphone from Samaira. "Thanks for the lovely, romantic performance, Samaira, we adored it. People, now it is the time for deciding who is the best of the best. Please vote for your favourite contestant out of these five brilliant singers," she reminded the audience.

Vivian lifted his mobile phone and showed it to her. "The first vote is mine, Sami!" he shouted and waved at her. The other contestants were invited to the stage. Laila gave the audience and the TV viewers exactly ten minutes to vote. Meanwhile, she entertained the crowd with funny anecdotes about the show and its contestants. There was a gigantic screen at the other end for people to get a proper look at the contestants who waited for their results with bated breath. Minutes ticked by.

Samaira had eyes only for Vivian. She was dying to know how he had come here. Digital counting was done by the Planet TV crew.

"I have the results with me," Laila tested the patience of the crowd.

They cheered with fervour, eager to know who was the winner.

"This has been a long but eventful journey for all our five contestants, but only one is going to claim the coveted title.

"Ladies and gentlemen, the moment you have been waiting for has arrived. I don't know the name of the winner yet; it is safe inside this cover. Let me pull the slip out for you," she created suspense amidst the audience. "Start counting, guys—ten, nine, eight, seven . . ."

Everyone had their hearts in their mouths. Vivian's heart pounded wildly.

"Three, two, one, and the winner is . . . Ms Samaira Ranjan!"

People cheered for her, and the stadium rocked with applause. The other contestants hugged her with joy. Samaira ran from the stage towards Vivian. The cameras and Laila followed.

Vivian met her halfway. She hugged him tight. She ran her hands over his face to make sure that he was indeed real. She touched his hair, his face, his eyelids . . .

"You are real!" she exclaimed.

"Yes, Sami, I am real," he confirmed.

"For a moment, I thought I imagined your presence." Her eyes filled with tears.

He half-smiled in response.

"Vivian, you came for me!" she cried, completely abandoning herself to him.

He hugged her back. "I promised you, Sami, and I kept the promise. I whistled and cheered for you," replied Vivian.

He held her cheeks tenderly and continued, "Your song was awesome . . . you deserve the title."

With that declaration, he took her in his arms and circled her with delight. She screamed her happiness to the world. "I love you, Viv! I am the happiest soul on earth right now!"

Raghu tried to stop Vivian. Barely out of the coma, he did not want his boss to strain himself. But Dr Bala held him back.

"Let him be himself. He is perfectly all right," he told Raghu, his eyes filled with tears.

Laila broke their embrace.

"Sorry to disturb these lovebirds, but I have to present this trophy to the winner."

Samaira accepted the trophy gracefully after Vivian released her.

"Your dance of joy told us a love story. Would you care to share a few words about your lover . . . or should I say your fiancée?" she amended herself as she noticed the diamond ring on Samaira's finger.

"Thanks, everyone!" She raised the trophy.

"Thanks to those who voted for me, and special thanks to those who criticised me as well. I hold this because of both." She indicated her trophy.

"But I have to once again thank that *one* person who is the reason behind this journey. There was a point when I felt hopeless and frustrated with life. I mocked at love, and survival was my only goal. That was when I met Vivian Andhera for the first time. He broke my walls . . . talked me out of my depression. He was the one who struggled for me and pushed me towards my dreams. He showed me what true love is. And I love you, Viv; you are the best!"

"Wow, that was an impressive speech. Ladies and gentlemen, a bigger round of applause for the guy behind our woman—Mr Vivian Andhera!" Laila cheered.

The audience went crazy, applauding and cheering them on. Raghu whispered something in her ears.

"Another good news for the couple. It is not just Samaira's day but also Vivian's. He has been named as the 'top entrepreneur' of this year."

Samaira put her hands over his cheeks. "I anticipated this!" she exclaimed with joy.

They hugged again, sharing the happiness of their success. *They had done it!*

"This is how love should be. Samaira saw his dream in her eyes, and Vivian saw hers in his. I wish this lovely couple every joy and happiness, for showing what true love is to this world," congratulated Laila.

***

Vivian walked into his room after a brief visit to his office. Samaira was busy packing her things.

"Where do you think you are going?" he demanded as he pulled her into his arms.

"You are perfectly fine. That is what Dr Bala told me." She took his hands and turned to face him.

"So?" He drew her into his clasp again.

"We are just engaged, Viv, not married. So, I must move out," she reminded him.

"Are you scared now that I am fine, I will have my naughty ways with you?" His eyes sparkled mischievously.

Samaira blushed at his possessive look. "Yes, I am."

"Ha-ha, should I wait for you for one more week?" He kissed her on her face.

"Yes, and that is your punishment for acting as if you were asleep this morning. You should have told me you were better. I was so worried," she complained.

"Ever since the accident, I could hear you. Your words made sense, but I was not able to respond. I could not even cry. I was not able to show you my feelings and emotions."

He continued, "It was a nightmare. Later, I could also feel your touch but couldn't react. My mind had no control over my body. Your kisses and songs brought me back, Sami."

She held his hands and squeezed them, reassuring herself that he was back in the world of the living. He had passed his toughest exam in life with flying colours.

"You fought for your life, Viv. You could not have done it if not for the fire inside you."

Vivian smiled. "Your words pushed me, Sami. Your writings on the display board inspired me. Your one-sided arguments won me over. You pulled me out of this rut. You are like my mother, Sami. You recreated the new Vivian," he said with gratitude.

"And you made Samaira Version 2.0."

He did not let her out of his grasp. "Over the past week I got back my reflexes gradually, but I did not want to show you, because I did not want to raise your hopes if I did not make further progress."

"That would never have happened. I know. You would have never given up," she said with certainty.

"When you reminded me about our promise on the balcony that day, I regained myself completely. I felt fine. I got back my reflexes. I wanted to hug you, but I did not react. I wanted to surprise you on your big day."

"Hah, you are a cheater, Vivian. I saw you turning in your sleep. I should have realised." She pushed at his chest and turned away in mock anger.

He caught her and whispered in her ears, "I love you, Sami."

With the declaration of his love, he trailed his lips down the back of her neck. She could feel his breath at her ear. This was the moment she had longed for. Her body trembled, acknowledging the heat of his kiss. Overcome by a wave of helplessness, she yielded to him. Passion overtook them. He turned her back towards him. Her legs wobbled; she would have fallen if not for his strong hold over her hips. Her vision blurred as he claimed her lips, at first gently and then fiercely possessive, telling her clearly, "*You are mine.*"

Wild tremors coursed through her, and she clung to him with an intensity that matched up to his. Their bodies entwined, he brought out dizzy sensations that she never knew existed within her. She traced his hands, and he tasted the sweetness of her honeyed lips.

Cupping his face, she kissed him fervently. Passion and tenderness engulfed them.

"Where is my *kulfi*?" he demanded.

"Let us go." She dragged him out of his room.

***

It was almost a year after their wedding. Today, Kushi was getting married to Amar. After a long struggle, Amar had convinced Kushi to marry him.

"You look gorgeous, Sami. All male eyes will be on you," he complained.

"But I have eyes only for you," she countered.

"I know that, and I love you for that, Mrs Andhera."

Samaira passed a gift to him. "This is for you, before we leave."

"Today is Kushi's wedding, not ours. Our anniversary is next week," he chided.

"I know that, but today is also a special day for us," she declared.

"Hah, the day you won the title," he recollected.

"And the day you topped the top ten entrepreneur list for the first time."

She patted his shoulder affectionately. Vivian opened the box to find a CD of her latest album.

"My love . . . by Samaira Andhera . . . for Vivian Andhera."

"I am proud of you, Sami."

"That's what I want!"

The crystal shaped as two thumbs that Vivian had gifted her earlier, now stood as a symbol of their love. Together, they had placed the heart back on it.

Their lips met in a tender gesture of love. Mr Andhera went back downstairs, smiling to himself. They needed their privacy to bring his granddaughter soon into this world. After all, the world was theirs!

THE BEGINNING

ABOUT THE AUTHOR

A university topper twice academically, Saranya Umakanthan is a software engineer by profession. With her novel, "*One Day, Life Will Change*" she has ventured into the world of inspiring romantic stories.

With her passion for writing, she wishes to leave an imprint in people's hearts, weaving beautiful stories with her words. A romantic by nature, Saranya loves gazing at the night sky while enjoying a cup of coffee. Nothing brings her more contentment than seeing a reader enjoy her book. The fragrance and texture of paperbacks inspire her and she hangs out at bookstores frequently. She would love to hear your feedback.

Email her at saranya.umakanthan@gmail.com.

Join her fan club, if you love her stories.

Instagram: https://www.instagram.com/saranya_umakanthan/
Facebook: https://www.facebook.com/authorsaranyaumakanthan/
Twitter: https://twitter.com/chayablossom